THE
CRYING OF
LOT 49

thomas pynchon

THE CRYING OF LOT 49

HARPER**PERENNIAL** ● MODERN**CLASSICS**

NEW YORK ● LONDON ● TORONTO ● SYDNEY ● NEW DELHI ● AUCKLAND

HARPER**PERENNIAL** ● MODERN**CLASSICS**

First PERENNIAL FICTION LIBRARY edition published 1986, reissued 1990; reissued in Perennial Classics 1999.

First Harper Perennial Modern Classics edition published 2006, reissued 2014.

The Library of Congress had catalogued the 1986 edition as follows:
Pynchon, Thomas
   The crying of lot 49 / Thomas Pynchon.
    p. cm.
   ISBN 0-06-091307-X
   1. Administration of estates—California—Fiction.
   2. Married women—California—Fiction. I. Title
   II. Title: Crying of lot forty-nine.
   PS3566.Y55C79 1986
   813'.54—dc19
   85-45221

ISBN: 978-0-06-233441-1
(Harper Perennial Deluxe Modern Classics edition)

    20 21 22 LSC 10 9 8 7 6

THE
CRYING OF
LOT 49

1

One summer afternoon Mrs Oedipa Maas came home from a Tupper-
ware party whose hostess had put perhaps too much kirsch in the
fondue to find that she, Oedipa, had been named executor, or
she supposed executrix, of the estate of one Pierce Inverarity, a
California real estate mogul who had once lost two million dollars
in his spare time but still had assets numerous and tangled enough
to make the job of sorting it all out more than honorary. Oedipa
stood in the living room, stared at by the greenish dead eye of the
TV tube, spoke the name of God, tried to feel as drunk as possible. But this did not work. She thought of a hotel room in
Mazatlán whose door had just been slammed, it seemed forever,
waking up two hundred birds down in the lobby; a sunrise over
the library slope at Cornell University that nobody out on it had
seen because the slope faces west; a dry, disconsolate tune from
the fourth movement of the Bartók Concerto for Orchestra; a
whitewashed bust of Jay Gould that Pierce kept over the bed on
a shelf so narrow for it she'd always had the hovering fear it would
someday topple on them. Was that how he'd died, she wondered,
among dreams, crushed by the only ikon in the house? That only

made her laugh, out loud and helpless: You're so sick, Oedipa, she told herself, or the room, which knew.

The letter was from the law firm of Warpe, Wistfull, Kubitschek and McMingus, of Los Angeles, and signed by somebody named Metzger. It said Pierce had died back in the spring, and they'd only just now found the will. Metzger was to act as co-executor and special counsel in the event of any involved litigation. Oedipa had been named also to execute the will in a codicil dated a year ago. She tried to think back to whether anything unusual had happened around then. Through the rest of the afternoon, through her trip to the market in downtown Kinneret-Among-The-Pines to buy ricotta and listen to the Muzak (today she came through the bead-curtained entrance around bar 4 of the Fort Wayne Settecento Ensemble's variorum recording of the Vivaldi Kazoo Concerto, Boyd Beaver, soloist); then through the sunned gathering of her marjoram and sweet basil from the herb garden, reading of book reviews in the latest *Scientific American*, into the layering of a lasagna, garlicking of a bread, tearing up of romaine leaves, eventually, oven on, into the mixing of the twilight's whiskey sours against the arrival of her husband, Wendell ("Mucho") Maas from work, she wondered, wondered, shuffling back through a fat deckful of days which seemed (wouldn't she be first to admit it?) more or less identical, or all pointing the same way subtly like a conjurer's deck, any odd one readily clear to a trained eye. It took her till the middle of Huntley and Brinkley to remember that last year at three or so one morning there had come this long-distance call, from where she would never know (unless now he'd left a diary) by a voice beginning in heavy Slavic tones as second secretary at the Transylvanian Consulate, looking for an escaped bat; modulated to comic-Negro, then on into hostile Pachuco dialect, full of chingas and maricones; then a Gestapo officer asking her in shrieks did she have relatives in

Germany and finally his Lamont Cranston voice, the one he'd talked in all the way down to Mazatlán. "Pierce, please," she'd managed to get in, "I thought we had——"

"But Margo," earnestly, "I've just come from Commissioner Weston, and that old man in the fun house was murdered by the same blowgun that killed Professor Quackenbush," or something.

"For God's sake," she said. Mucho had rolled over and was looking at her.

"Why don't you hang up on him," Mucho suggested, sensibly.

"I heard that," Pierce said. "I think it's time Wendell Maas had a little visit from The Shadow." Silence, positive and thorough, fell. So it was the last of his voices she ever heard. Lamont Cranston. That phone line could have pointed any direction, been any length. Its quiet ambiguity shifted over, in the months after the call, to what had been revived: memories of his face, body, things he'd given her, things she had now and then pretended not to've heard him say. It took him over, and to the verge of being forgotten. The shadow waited a year before visiting. But now there was Metzger's letter. Had Pierce called last year then to tell her about this codicil? Or had he decided on it later, somehow because of her annoyance and Mucho's indifference? She felt exposed, finessed, put down. She had never executed a will in her life, didn't know where to begin, didn't know how to tell the law firm in L. A. that she didn't know where to begin.

"Mucho, baby," she cried, in an access of helplessness.

Mucho Maas, home, bounded through the screen door. "Today was another defeat," he began.

"Let me tell you," she also began. But let Mucho go first.

He was a disk jockey who worked further along the Peninsula and suffered regular crises of conscience about his profession.

"I don't believe in any of it, Oed," he could usually get out. "I try, I truly can't," way down there, further down perhaps than she could reach, so that such times often brought her near panic. It might have been the sight of her so about to lose control that seemed to bring him back up.

"You're too sensitive." Yeah, there was so much else she ought to be saying also, but this was what came out. It was true, anyway. For a couple years he'd been a used car salesman and so hyperaware of what *that* profession had come to mean that working hours were exquisite torture to him. Mucho shaved his upper lip every morning three times with, three times against the grain to remove any remotest breath of a moustache, new blades he drew blood invariably but kept at it; bought all natural-shoulder suits, then went to a tailor to have the lapels made yet more abnormally narrow, on his hair used only water, combing it like Jack Lemmon to throw them further off. The sight of sawdust, even pencil shavings, made him wince, his own kind being known to use it for hushing sick transmissions, and though he dieted he could still not as Oedipa did use honey to sweeten his coffee for like all things viscous it distressed him, recalling too poignantly what is often mixed with motor oil to ooze dishonest into gaps between piston and cylinder wall. He walked out of a party one night because somebody used the word "creampuff," it seemed maliciously, in his hearing. The man was a refugee Hungarian pastry cook talking shop, but there was your Mucho: thin-skinned.

Yet at least he had believed in the cars. Maybe to excess: how could he not, seeing people poorer than him come in, Negro, Mexican, cracker, a parade seven days a week, bringing the most godawful of trade-ins: motorized, metal extensions of themselves, of their families and what their whole lives must be like, out there so naked for anybody, a stranger like himself, to look at, frame cockeyed, rusty underneath, fender repainted in a shade just off enough to depress the value, if not Mucho himself, inside smelling hopelessly of children, supermarket booze, two, sometimes three generations of cigarette smokers, or only of dust—and when the cars were swept out you had to look at the actual residue of these lives, and there was no way of telling what things had been truly refused (when so little he supposed came by that out of fear most of it had to be taken and kept) and what had simply (perhaps tragically) been lost: clipped coupons promising savings of 5 or 10¢, trading stamps, pink flyers advertising specials at the markets, butts, tooth-shy combs, help-wanted ads, Yellow Pages torn from the phone book, rags of old underwear or dresses that already were period costumes, for wiping your own breath off the inside of a windshield with so you could see whatever it was, a movie, a woman or car you coveted, a cop who might pull you over just for drill, all the bits and pieces coated uniformly, like a salad of despair, in a gray dressing of ash, condensed exhaust, dust, body wastes—it made him sick to look, but he had to look. If it had been an outright junkyard, probably he could have stuck things out, made a career: the violence that had caused each wreck being infrequent enough, far enough away from him, to be miraculous, as each death, up till the moment of our own, is miraculous. But the endless rituals of trade-in, week after week, never got as far as violence or blood, and so were too plausible for the impressionable Mucho to take for long. Even if enough exposure to the unvarying gray sickness had somehow managed to immunize him, he could still never accept the way each owner, each shadow, filed in only to exchange a dented, malfunctioning version of himself for another, just as futureless, automotive projection of somebody else's life. As if it were the most natural thing. To Mucho it was horrible. Endless, convoluted incest.

Oedipa couldn't understand how he could still get so upset

even now. By the time he married her he'd already been two years at the station, KCUF, and the lot on the pallid, roaring arterial was far behind him, like the Second World or Korean Wars were for older husbands. Maybe, God help her, he should have been in a war, Japs in trees, Krauts in Tiger tanks, gooks with trumpets in the night he might have forgotten sooner than whatever it was about the lot that had stayed so alarmingly with him for going on five years. Five years. You comfort them when they wake pouring sweat or crying out in the language of bad dreams, yes, you hold them, they calm down, one day they lose it: she knew that. But when was Mucho going to forget? She suspected the disk jockey spot (which he'd got through his good buddy the KCUF advertising manager, who'd visited the lot once a week, the lot being a sponsor) was a way of letting the Top 200, and even the news copy that came jabbering out of the machine—all the fraudulent dream of teenage appetites—be a buffer between him and that lot.

He had believed too much in the lot, he believed not at all in the station. Yet to look at him now, in the twilit living room, gliding like a large bird in an updraft toward the sweating shakerful of booze, smiling out of his fat vortex ring's center, you'd think all was flat calm, gold, serene.

Until he opened his mouth. "Today Funch," he told her, pouring, "had me in, wanted to talk about my image, which he doesn't like." Funch being the program director, and Mucho's great foe. "I'm too horny, now. What I should be is a young father, a big brother. These little chicks call in with requests, naked lust, to Funch's ear, throbs in every word I say. So now I'm suppose to tape all the phone talk, Funch personally will edit out anything he considers offensive, meaning all of my end of the conversation. Censorship, I told him, 'fink,' I muttered, and fled." He and Funch went through some such routine maybe once a week.

She showed him the letter from Metzger. Mucho knew all about her and Pierce: it had ended a year before Mucho married her. He read the letter and withdrew along a shy string of eye-blinks.

"What am I going to do?" she said.

"Oh, no," said Mucho, "you got the wrong fella. Not me. I can't even make out our income tax right. Execute a will, there's nothing I can tell you, see Roseman." Their lawyer.

"Mucho. Wendell. It was *over*. *Before* he put my name on it."

"Yeah, yeah. I meant only that, Oed. I'm not capable."

So next morning that's what she did, went and saw Roseman. After a half hour in front of her vanity mirror drawing and having to redraw dark lines along her eyelids that each time went ragged or wavered violently before she could take the brush away. She'd been up most of the night, after another three-in-the-morning phone call, its announcing bell clear cardiac terror, so out of nothing did it come, the instrument one second inert, the next screaming. It brought both of them instantly awake and they lay, joints unlocking, not even wanting to look at each other for the first few rings. She finally, having nothing she knew of to lose, had taken it. It was Dr Hilarius, her shrink or psychotherapist. But he sounded like Pierce doing a Gestapo officer.

"I didn't wake you up, did I," he began, dry. "You sound so frightened. How are the pills, not working?"

"I'm not taking them," she said.

"You feel threatened by them?"

"I don't know what's inside them."

"You don't believe that they're only tranquilizers."

"Do I trust you?" She didn't, and what he said next explained why not.

"We still need a hundred-and-fourth for the bridge." Chuckled aridly. The bridge, die Brücke, being his pet name for the experiment he was helping the community hospital run on effects of LSD-25, mescaline, psilocybin, and related drugs on a large sample of surburban housewives. The bridge inward. "When can you let us fit you into our schedule."

"No," she said, "you have half a million others to choose from. It's three in the morning."

"We want you." Hanging in the air over her bed she now beheld the well-known portrait of Uncle that appears in front of all our post offices, his eyes gleaming unhealthily, his sunken yellow cheeks most violently rouged, his finger pointing between her eyes. I want you. She had never asked Dr Hilarius why, being afraid of all he might answer.

"I am having a hallucination now, I don't need drugs for that."

"Don't describe it," he said quickly. "Well. Was there anything else you wanted to talk about."

"Did I call you?"

"I thought so," he said, "I had this feeling. Not telepathy. But rapport with a patient is a curious thing sometimes."

"Not this time." She hung up. And then couldn't get to sleep. But would be damned if she'd take the capsules he'd given her. Literally damned. She didn't want to get hooked in any way, she'd told him that.

"So," he shrugged, "on me you are not hooked? Leave then. You're cured."

She didn't leave. Not that the shrink held any dark power over her. But it was easier to stay. Who'd know the day she was cured? Not him, he'd admitted that himself. "Pills are different," she pleaded. Hilarius only made a face at her, one he'd made before. He was full of these delightful lapses from orthodoxy. His theory being that a face is symmetrical like a Rorschach blot, tells a story like a TAT picture, excites a response like a suggested word, so why not. He claimed to have once cured a case of hysterical blindness with his number 37, the "Fu-Manchu" (many of the faces having like German symphonies both a number and nickname), which involved slanting the eyes up with the index fingers, enlarging the nostrils with the middle fingers, pulling the mouth wide with the pinkies and protruding the tongue. On Hilarius it was truly alarming. And in fact, as Oedipa's Uncle Sam hallucination faded, it was this Fu-Manchu face that came dissolving in to replace it and stay with her for what was left of the hours before dawn. It put her in hardly any shape to see Roseman.

But Roseman had also spent a sleepless night, brooding over the Perry Mason television program the evening before, which his wife was fond of but toward which Roseman cherished a fierce ambivalence, wanting at once to be a successful trial lawyer like Perry Mason and, since this was impossible, to destroy Perry Mason by undermining him. Oedipa walked in more or less by surprise to catch her trusted family lawyer stuffing with guilty haste a wad of different-sized and colored papers into a desk drawer. She knew it was the rough draft of *The Profession v. Perry Mason, A Not-so-hypothetical Indictment,* and had been in progress for as long as the TV show had been on the air.

"You didn't use to look guilty, as I remember," Oedipa said. They often went to the same group therapy sessions, in a car pool with a photographer from Palo Alto who thought he was a volleyball. "That's a good sign, isn't it?"

"You might have been one of Perry Mason's spies," said Roseman. After thinking a moment he added, "Ha, ha."

"Ha, ha," said Oedipa. They looked at each other. "I have to execute a will," she said.

"Oh, go ahead then," said Roseman, "don't let me keep you."

"No," said Oedipa, and told him all.

"Why would he do a thing like that," Roseman puzzled, after reading the letter.

"You mean die?"

"No," said Roseman, "name you to help execute it."

"He was unpredictable." They went to lunch. Roseman tried to play footsie with her under the table. She was wearing boots, and couldn't feel much of anything. So, insulated, she decided not to make any fuss.

"Run away with me," said Roseman when the coffee came.

"Where?" she asked. That shut him up.

Back in the office, he outlined what she was in for: learn intimately the books and the business, go through probate, collect all debts, inventory the assets, get an appraisal of the estate, decide what to liquidate and what to hold on to, pay off claims, square away taxes, distribute legacies . . .

"Hey," said Oedipa, "can't I get somebody to do it for me?"

"Me," said Roseman, "some of it, sure. But aren't you even interested?"

"In what?"

"In what you might find out."

As things developed, she was to have all manner of revelations. Hardly about Pierce Inverarity, or herself; but about what remained yet had somehow, before this, stayed away. There had hung the sense of buffering, insulation, she had noticed the absence of an intensity, as if watching a movie, just perceptibly out of focus, that the projectionist refused to fix. And had also gently conned herself into the curious, Rapunzel-like role of a pensive girl somehow, magically, prisoner among the pines and salt fogs of Kinneret, looking for somebody to say hey, let down your hair. When it turned out to be Pierce she'd happily pulled out the pins and curlers and down it tumbled in its whispering, dainty avalanche, only when Pierce had got maybe halfway up, her lovely hair turned, through some sinister sorcery, into a great unanchored wig, and down he fell, on his ass. But dauntless, perhaps using one of his many credit cards for a shim, he'd slipped the lock on her tower door and come up the conchlike stairs, which, had true guile come more naturally to him, he'd have done to begin with. But all that had then gone on between them had really never escaped the confinement of that tower. In Mexico City they somehow wandered into an exhibition of paintings by the beautiful Spanish exile Remedios Varo: in the central painting of a triptych, titled "Bordando el Manto Terrestre," were a number of frail girls with heart-shaped faces, huge eyes, spun-gold hair, prisoners in the top room of a circular tower, embroidering a kind of tapestry which spilled out the slit windows and into a void, seeking hopelessly to fill the void: for all the other buildings and creatures, all the waves, ships and forests of the earth were contained in this tapestry, and the tapestry was the world. Oedipa, perverse, had stood in front of the painting and cried. No one had noticed; she wore dark green bubble shades. For a moment she'd wondered if the seal around her sockets were tight enough to allow the tears simply to go on and fill up the entire lens space and never dry. She could carry the sadness of the moment with her that way forever, see the world refracted through those tears, those specific tears, as if indices as yet unfound varied in important ways from cry to cry. She had looked down at her feet and known, then, because of a painting, that what she stood on had only been woven together a couple thousand miles away in her own tower, was only by accident known as Mexico, and so Pierce had taken her away from nothing, there'd been no escape. What did she so desire escape from? Such a captive maiden, having plenty of time to think, soon realizes that her tower, its height and architecture, are like her ego only incidental: that what really keeps her where she is is magic, anonymous and malignant, visited on her from outside and for no reason at all. Having no apparatus except gut fear and female cunning to examine this formless magic, to understand how it works, how to measure its field strength, count its lines of force, she may fall back on superstition, or take up a useful hobby like embroidery, or go mad, or marry a disk jockey. If the tower is everywhere and the knight of deliverance no proof against its magic, what else?

2

She left Kinneret, then, with no idea she was moving toward anything new. Mucho Maas, enigmatic, whistling "I Want to Kiss Your Feet," a new recording by Sick Dick and the Volkswagens (an English group he was fond of at that time but did not believe in), stood with hands in pockets while she explained about going down to San Narciso for a while to look into Pierce's books and records and confer with Metzger, the coexecutor. Mucho was sad to see her go, but not desperate, so after telling him to hang up if Dr. Hilarius called and look after the oregano in the garden, which had contracted a strange mold, she went.

San Narciso lay further south, near L.A. Like many named places in California it was less an identifiable city than a grouping of concepts—census tracts, special purpose bond-issue districts, shopping nuclei, all overlaid with access roads to its own freeway. But it had been Pierce's domicile, and headquarters: the place he'd begun his land speculating in ten years ago, and so put down the plinth course of capital on which everything afterward had been built, however rickety or grotesque, toward the sky; and that, she supposed, would set the spot apart, give it an aura. But if there was any vital difference between it and the rest of Southern California, it was invisible on first glance. She drove into San Narciso on a Sunday, in a rented Impala. Nothing was happening. She looked down a slope, needing to squint for the sunlight, onto a vast sprawl of houses which had grown up all together, like a well-tended crop, from the dull brown earth; and she thought of the time she'd opened a transistor radio to replace a battery and seen her first printed circuit. The ordered swirl of houses and streets, from this high angle, sprang at her now with the same unexpected, astonishing clarity as the circuit card had. Though she knew even less about radios than about Southern Californians, there were to both outward patterns a hieroglyphic sense of concealed meaning, of an intent to communicate. There'd seemed no limit to what the printed circuit could have told her (if she had tried to find out); so in her first minute of San Narciso, a revelation also trembled just past the threshold of her understanding. Smog hung all round the horizon, the sun on the bright beige countryside was painful; she and the Chevy seemed parked at the centre of an odd, religious instant. As if, on some other frequency, or out of the eye of some whirlwind rotating too slow for her heated skin even to feel the centrifugal coolness of, words were being spoken. She suspected that much. She thought of Mucho, her husband, trying to believe in his job. Was it something like this he felt, looking through the soundproof glass at one of his colleagues with a headset clamped on and cueing the next record with movements stylized as the handling of chrism, censer, chalice might be for a holy man, yet really tuned in to the voice, voices, the music, its message, surrounded by it, digging it, as were all the faithful it went out to; did Mucho stand outside Studio A looking in, knowing that even if he could hear it he couldn't believe in it?

She gave it up presently, as if a cloud had approached the

sun or the smog thickened, and so broken the "religious instant," whatever it might've been; started up and proceeded at maybe 70 mph along the singing blacktop, onto a highway she thought went toward Los Angeles, into a neighborhood that was little more than the road's skinny right-of-way, lined by auto lots, escrow services, drive-ins, small office buildings and factories whose address numbers were in the 70 and then 80,000's. She had never known numbers to run so high. It seemed unnatural. To her left appeared a prolonged scatter of wide, pink buildings, surrounded by miles of fence topped with barbed wire and inter-rupted now and then by guard towers: soon an entrance whizzed by, two sixty-foot missiles on either side and the name YOYODYNE lettered conservatively on each nose cone. This was San Narciso's big source of employment, the Galactronics Division of Yoyo-dyne, Inc., one of the giants of the aerospace industry. Pierce, she happened to know, had owned a large block of shares, had been somehow involved in negotiating an understanding with the county tax assessor to lure Yoyodyne here in the first place. It was part, he explained, of being a founding father.

Barbed wire again gave way to the familiar parade of more beige, prefab, cinderblock office machine distributors, sealant makers, bottled gas works, fastener factories, warehouses, and whatever. Sunday had sent them all into silence and paralysis, all but an occasional real estate office or truck stop. Oedipa resolved to pull in at the next motel she saw, however ugly, stillness and four walls having at some point become preferable to this illusion of speed, freedom, wind in your hair, unreeling landscape—it wasn't. What the road really was, she fancied, was this hypoder-mic needle, inserted somewhere ahead into the vein of a freeway, a vein nourishing the mainliner L.A., keeping it happy, coherent, protected from pain, or whatever passes, with a city, for pain. But were Oedipa some single melted crystal of urban horse, L.A., really, would be no less turned on for her absence.

Still, when she got a look at the next motel, she hesitated a second. A representation in painted sheet metal of a nymph holding a white blossom towered thirty feet into the air; the sign, lit up despite the sun, said "Echo Courts." The face of the nymph was much like Oedipa's, which didn't startle her so much as a concealed blower system that kept the nymph's gauze chiton in constant agitation, revealing enormous vermilion-tipped breasts and long pink thighs at each flap. She was smiling a lipsticked and public smile, not quite a hooker's but nowhere near that of any nymph pining away with love either. Oedipa pulled into the lot, got out and stood for a moment in the hot sun and the dead-still air, watching the artificial windstorm overhead toss gauze in five-foot excursions. Remembering her idea about a slow whirlwind, words she couldn't hear.

The room would be good enough for the time she had to stay. Its door opened on a long courtyard with a swimming pool, whose surface that day was flat, brilliant with sunlight. At the far end stood a fountain, with another nymph. Nothing moved. If people lived behind the other doors or watched through the windows gagged each with its roaring air-conditioner, she couldn't see them. The manager, a drop-out named Miles, maybe 16 with a Beatle haircut and a lapelless, cuffless, one-button mohair suit, carried her bags and sang to himself, possibly to her:

MILES'S SONG

Too fat to Frug,
That's what you tell me all the time,
When you really try'n' to put me down,
But I'm hip,
So close your big fat lip,
Yeah, baby,
I may be too fat to Frug,
But at least I ain't too slim to Swim.

"It's lovely," said Oedipa, "but why do you sing with an English accent when you don't talk that way?"

"It's this group I'm in," Miles explained, "the Paranoids. We're new yet. Our manager says we should sing like that. We watch English movies a lot, for the accent."

"My husband's a disk jockey," Oedipa trying to be helpful, "it's only a thousand-watt station, but if you had anything like a tape I could give it to him to plug."

Miles closed the door behind them and started in with the shifty eye. "In return for what?" Moving in on her. "Do you want what I think you want? This is the Payola Kid here, you know." Oedipa picked up the nearest weapon, which happened to be the rabbit-ear antenna off the TV in the corner. "Oh," said Miles, stopping. "You hate me too." Eyes bright through his bangs.

"You *are* a paranoid," Oedipa said.

"I have a smooth young body," said Miles, "I thought you older chicks went for that." He left after shaking her down for four bits for carrying the bags.

That night the lawyer Metzger showed up. He turned out to be so good-looking that Oedipa thought at first They, somebody up there, were putting her on. It had to be an actor. He stood at her door, behind him the oblong pool shimmering silent in a mild diffusion of light from the nighttime sky, saying, "Mrs. Maas," like a reproach. His enormous eyes, lambent, extravagantly lashed, smiled out at her wickedly; she looked around him for reflectors, microphones, camera cabling, but there was only himself and a debonair bottle of French Beaujolais, which he claimed to've smuggled last year into California, this rollicking law-breaker, past the frontier guards.

"So hey," he murmured, "after scouring motels all day to find you, I can come in there, can't I?"

Oedipa had planned on nothing more involved that evening

than watching *Bonanza* on the tube. She'd shifted into stretch denim slacks and a shaggy black sweater, and had her hair all the way down. She knew she looked pretty good. "Come in," she said, "but I only have one glass."

"I," the gallant Metzger let her know, "can drink out of the bottle." He came in and sat on the floor, in his suit. Opened the bottle, poured her a drink, began to talk. It presently came out that Oedipa hadn't been so far off, thinking it was an actor. Some twenty-odd years ago, Metzger had been one of those child movie stars, performing under the name of Baby Igor. "My mother," he announced bitterly, "was really out to kasher me, boy, like a piece of beef on the sink, she wanted me drained and white. Times I wonder," smoothing down the hair at the back of his head, "if she succeeded. It scares me. You know what mothers like that turn their male children into."

"You certainly don't look," Oedipa began, then had second thoughts.

Metzger flashed her a big wry couple rows of teeth. "Looks don't mean a thing any more," he said. "I live inside my looks, and I'm never sure. The possibility haunts me."

"And how often," Oedipa inquired, now aware it was all words, "has that line of approach worked for you, Baby Igor?"

"Do you know," Metzger said, "Inverarity only mentioned you to me once."

"Were you close?"

"No. I drew up his will. Don't you want to know what he said?"

"No," said Oedipa, and snapped on the television set. Onto the screen bloomed the image of a child of indeterminate sex, its bare legs pressed awkward together, its shoulder-length curls mingling with the shorter hair of a St. Bernard, whose long tongue, as Oedipa watched, began to swipe at the child's rosy cheeks, making the child wrinkle up its nose appealingly and say, "Aw, Murray, come on, now, you're getting me all wet."

"That's me, that's me," cried Metzger, staring, "good God."

"Which one?" asked Oedipa.

"That movie was called," Metzger snapped his fingers, "*Cashiered.*"

"About you and your mother."

"About this kid and his father, who's drummed out of the British Army for cowardice, only he's covering up for a friend, see, and to redeem himself he and the kid follow the old regiment to Gallipoli, where the father somehow builds a midget submarine, and every week they slip through the Dardanelles into the Sea of Marmara and torpedo the Turkish merchantmen, the father, son, and St Bernard. The dog sits on periscope watch, and barks if he sees anything."

Oedipa was pouring wine. "You're kidding."

"Listen, listen, here's where I sing." And sure enough, the child, and dog, and a merry old Greek fisherman who had appeared from nowhere with a zither, now all stood in front of phony-Dodecanese process footage of a seashore at sunset, and the kid sang.

Baby Igor's Song

'Gainst the Hun and the Turk, never once do we shirk,
My daddy, my doggie and me.
Through the perilous years, like the Three Musketeers,
We will stick just as close as can be.
Soon our sub's periscope'll aim for Constantinople,
As again we set hopeful to sea;
Once more unto the breach, for those boys on the beach,
Just my daddy, my doggie and me.

Then there was a musical bridge, featuring the fisherman and his instrument, then the young Metzger took it from the top while his aging double, over Oedipa's protests, sang harmony.

Either he made up the whole thing, Oedipa thought suddenly, or he bribed the engineer over at the local station to run this, it's all part of a plot, an elaborate, seduction, *plot*. O Metzger.

"You didn't sing along," he observed.

"I didn't *know*," Oedipa smiled. On came a loud commercial for Fangoso Lagoons, a new housing development west of here.

"One of Inverarity's interests," Metzger noted. It was to be laced by canals with private landings for power boats, a floating social hall in the middle of an artificial lake, at the bottom of which lay restored galleons, imported from the Bahamas; Atlantean fragments of columns and friezes from the Canaries; real human skeletons from Italy; giant clamshells from Indonesia—all for the entertainment of Scuba enthusiasts. A map of the place flashed onto the screen, Oedipa drew a sharp breath, Metzger on the chance it might be for him looked over. But she'd only been reminded of her look downhill this noontime. Some immediacy was there again, some promise of hierophany: printed circuit, gently curving streets, private access to the water, Book of the Dead. . . .

Before she was ready for it, back came *Cashiered*. The little submarine, named the "Justine" after the dead mother, was at the quai, singling up all lines. A small crowd was seeing it off, among them the old fisherman, and his daughter, a leggy, ringletted nymphet who, should there be a happy ending, would end up with Metzger; an English missionary nurse with a nice build on her, who would end up with Metzger's father; and even a female sheepdog with eyes for Murray the St. Bernard.

"Oh, yeah," Metzger said, "this is where we have trouble in the Narrows. It's a bitch because of the Kephez minefields, but

Jerry has also recently hung this net, this gigantic net, woven out of cable 2½ inches thick."

Oedipa refilled her wine glass. They lay now, staring at the screen, flanks just lightly touching. There came from the TV set a terrific explosion. "Mines!" cried Metzger, covering his head and rolling away from her. "Daddy," blubbered the Metzger in the tube, "I'm scared." The inside of the midget sub was chaotic, the dog galloping to and fro scattering saliva that mingled with the spray from a leak in the bulkhead, which the father was now plugging with his shirt. "One thing we can do," announced the father, "go to the bottom, try to get *under* the net."

"Ridiculous," said Metzger. "They'd built a gate in it, so German U-boats could get through to attack the British fleet. All our E class subs simply used that gate."

"How do you know that?"

"Wasn't I there?"

"But," began Oedipa, then saw how they were suddenly out of wine.

"Aha," said Metzger, from an inside coat pocket producing a bottle of tequila.

"No lemons?" she asked, with movie-gaiety. "No salt?"

"A tourist thing. Did Inverarity use lemons when you were there?"

"How did you know we were there?" She watched him fill her glass, growing more anti-Metzger as the level rose.

"He wrote it off that year as a business expense. I did his tax stuff."

"A cash nexus," brooded Oedipa, "you and Perry Mason, two of a kind, it's all you know about, you shysters."

"But our beauty lies," explained Metzger, "in this extended capacity for convolution. A lawyer in a courtroom, in front of any jury, becomes an actor, right? Raymond Burr is an actor, impersonating a lawyer, who in front of a jury becomes an actor. Me, I'm a former actor who became a lawyer. They've done the pilot film of a TV series, in fact, based loosely on my career, starring my friend Manny Di Presso, a one-time lawyer who quit his firm to become an actor. Who in this pilot plays me, an actor become a lawyer reverting periodically to being an actor. The film is in an air-conditioned vault at one of the Hollywood studios, light can't fatigue it, it can be repeated endlessly."

"You're in trouble," Oedipa told him, staring at the tube, conscious of his thigh, warm through his suit and her slacks. Presently:

"The Turks are up there with searchlights," he said, pouring more tequila, watching the little submarine fill up, "patrol boats, and machine guns. You want to bet on what'll happen?"

"Of course not," said Oedipa, "the movie's made." He only smiled back. "One of your endless repetitions."

"But you still don't know," Metzger said. "You haven't seen it." Into the commercial break now roared a deafening ad for Beaconsfield Cigarettes, whose attractiveness lay in their filter's use of bone charcoal, the very best kind.

"Bones of what?" wondered Oedipa.

"Inverarity knew. He owned 51% of the filter process."

"Tell me."

"Someday. Right now it's your last chance to place your bet. Are they going to get out of it, or not?"

She felt drunk. It occurred to her, for no reason, that the plucky trio might not get out after all. She had no way to tell how long the movie had to run. She looked at her watch, but it had stopped. "This is absurd," she said, "of course they'll get out."

"How do you know?"

"All those movies had happy endings."

"All?"

"Most."

"That cuts down the probability," he told her, smug.

She squinted at him through her glass. "Then give me odds."

"Odds would give it away."

"So," she yelled, maybe a bit rattled, "I bet a bottle of something. Tequila, all right? That you didn't make it." Feeling the words had been conned out of her.

"That I didn't make it." He pondered. "Another bottle tonight would put you to sleep," he decided. "No."

"What do you want to bet, then?" She knew. Stubborn, they watched each other's eyes for what seemed five minutes. She heard commercials chasing one another into and out of the speaker of the TV. She grew more and more angry, perhaps juiced, perhaps only impatient for the movie to come back on.

"Fine then," she gave in at last, trying for a brittle voice, "it's a bet. Whatever you'd like. That you don't make it. That you all turn to carrion for the fish at the bottom of the Dardanelles, your daddy, your doggie, and you."

"Fair enough," drawled Metzger, taking her hand as if to shake on the bet and kissing its palm instead, sending the dry end of his tongue to graze briefly among her fate's furrows, the changeless salt hatchings of her identity. She wondered then if this were really happening in the same way as, say, her first time in bed with Pierce, the dead man. But then the movie came back.

The father was huddled in a shellhole on the steep cliffs of the Anzac beachhead, Turkish shrapnel flying all over the place. Neither Baby Igor nor Murray the dog were in evidence. "Now what the hell," said Oedipa.

"Golly," Metzger said, "they must have got the reels screwed up."

"Is this before or after?" she asked, reaching for the tequila bottle, a move that put her left breast in the region of Metzger's nose. The irrepressibly comic Metzger made crosseyes before replying,

"That would be telling."

"Come on." She nudged his nose with the padded tip of her bra cup and poured booze. "Or the bet's off."

"Nope," Metzger said.

"At least tell me if that's his old regiment, there."

"Go ahead," said Metzger, "ask questions. But for each answer, you'll have to take something off. We'll call it Strip Botticelli."

Oedipa had a marvellous idea: "Fine," she told him, "but first I'll just slip into the bathroom for a second. Close your eyes, turn around, don't peek." On the screen the "River Clyde," a collier carrying 2000 men, beached at Sedd-el-Bahr in an unearthly silence. "This is it, men," a phony British accent was heard to whisper. Suddenly a host of Turkish rifles on shore opened up all together, and the massacre began.

"I know this part," Metzger told her, his eyes squeezed shut, head away from the set. "For fifty yards out the sea was red with blood. They don't show that." Oedipa skipped into the bathroom, which happened also to have a walk-in closet, quickly undressed and began putting on as much as she could of the clothing she'd brought with her: six pairs of panties in assorted colors, girdle, three pairs of nylons, three brassieres, two pairs stretch slacks, four half-slips, one black sheath, two summer dresses, half dozen A-line skirts, three sweaters, two blouses, quilted wrapper, baby blue peignoir and old Orlon muu-muu. Bracelets then, scatterpins, earrings, a pendant. It all seemed to take hours to put on and she could hardly walk when she was finished. She made the mistake of looking at herself in the full-length mirror, saw a beach ball with feet, and laughed so violently she fell over, taking a can of hair spray on the sink with her. The can hit the floor, something broke, and with a great outsurge of pressure the stuff commenced atomizing, propelling the can swiftly about the bathroom. Metzger rushed in to find Oedipa rolling around, trying to get back on her feet, amid a great sticky miasma of fragrant lacquer. "Oh, for Pete's sake," he said in his Baby Igor voice. The can, hissing malignantly, bounced off the toilet and whizzed by Metzger's right ear, missing by maybe a quarter of an inch. Metzger hit the deck and cowered with Oedipa as the can continued its high-speed caroming; from the other room came a slow, deep crescendo of naval bombardment, machine-gun, howitzer and small-arms fire, screams and chopped-off prayers of dying infantry. She looked up past his eyelids, into the staring ceiling light, her field of vision cut across by wild, flashing overflights of the can, whose pressure seemed inexhaustible. She was scared but nowhere near sober. The can knew where it was going, she sensed, or something fast enough, God or a digital machine, might have computed in advance the complex web of its travel; but she wasn't fast enough, and knew only that it might hit them at any moment, at whatever clip it was doing, a hundred miles an hour. "Metzger," she moaned, and sank her teeth into his upper arm, through the sharkskin. Everything smelled like hair spray. The can collided with a mirror and bounced away, leaving a silvery, reticulated bloom of glass to hang a second before it all fell jingling into the sink; zoomed over to the enclosed shower, where it crashed into and totally destroyed a panel of frosted glass; thence around the three tile walls, up to the ceiling, past the light, over the two prostrate bodies, amid its own whoosh and the buzzing, distorted uproar from the TV set. She could imagine no end to it; yet presently the can did give up in midflight and fall to the floor, about a foot from Oedipa's nose. She lay watching it.

"Blimey," somebody remarked. "Coo." Oedipa took her teeth out of Metzger, looked around and saw in the doorway

Miles, the kid with the bangs and mohair suit, now multiplied by four. It seemed to be the group he'd mentioned, the Paranoids. She couldn't tell them apart, three of them were carrying electric guitars, they all had their mouth open. There also appeared a number of girls' faces, gazing through armpits and around angles of knees. "That's kinky," said one of the girls.

"Are you from London?" another wanted to know: "Is that a London thing you're doing?" Hair spray hung like fog, glass twinkled all over the floor.

"Lord love a duck," summarized a boy holding a passkey, and Oedipa decided this was Miles. Deferent, he began to narrate for their entertainment a surfer orgy he had been to the week before, involving a five-gallon can of kidney suet, a small automobile with a sun roof, and a trained seal.

"I'm sure this pales by comparison," said Oedipa, who'd succeeded in rolling over, "so why don't you all just, you know, go outside. And sing. None of this works without mood music. Serenade us."

"Maybe later," invited one of the other Paranoids shyly, "you could join us in the pool."

"Depends how hot it gets in here, gang," winked jolly Oedipa. The kids filed out, after plugging extension cords into all available outlets in the other room and leading them in a bundle out a window.

Metzger helped her stagger to her feet. "Anyone for Strip Botticelli?" In the other room the TV was blaring a commercial for a Turkish bath in downtown San Narciso, wherever downtown was, called Hogan's Seraglio. "Inverarity owned that too," Metzger said. "Did you know that?"

"Sadist," Oedipa yelled, "say it once more, I'll wrap the TV tube around your head."

"You're really mad," he smiled.

She wasn't, really. She said, "What the hell didn't he own?"
Metzger cocked an eyebrow at her. "You tell me."

If she was going to she got no chance, for outside, all in a shuddering deluge of thick guitar chords, the Paranoids had broken into song. Their drummer had set up precariously on the diving board, the others were invisible. Metzger came up behind her with some idea of cupping his hands around her breasts, but couldn't immediately find them because of all the clothes. They stood at the window and heard the Paranoids singing.

SERENADE

As I lie and watch the moon
On the lonely sea,
Watch it tug the lonely tide
Like a comforter over me,
The still and faceless moon
Fills the beach tonight
With only a ghost of day,
All shadow gray, and moonbeam white.
And you lie alone tonight,
As alone as I;
Lonely girl in your lonely flat, well, that's where it's at,
So hush your lonely cry.
How can I come to you, put out the moon, send back the tide?
The night has gone so gray, I'd lose the way, and it's dark inside.
No, I must lie alone,
Till it comes for me;
Till it takes the sky, the sand, the moon, and the lonely sea.
And the lonely sea . . . etc. [FADE OUT.]

"Now then," Oedipa shivered brightly.

"First question," Metzger reminded her. From the TV set the St Bernard was barking. Oedipa looked and saw Baby Igor, disguised as a Turkish beggar lad, skulking with the dog around a set she took to be Constantinople.

"Another early reel," she said hopefully.

"I can't allow that question," Metzger said. On the doorsill the Paranoids, as we leave milk to propitiate the leprechaun, had set a fifth of Jack Daniels.

"Oboy," said Oedipa. She poured a drink. "Did Baby Igor get to Constantinople in the good submarine 'Justine'?"

"No," said Metzger. Oedipa took off an earring.

"Did he get there in, what did you call them, in an E Class submarine."

"No," said Metzger. Oedipa took off another earring.

"Did he get there overland, maybe through Asia Minor?"

"Maybe," said Metzger. Oedipa took off another earring.

"Another earring?" said Metzger.

"If I answer that, will you take something off?"

"I'll do it without an answer," roared Metzger, shucking out of his coat. Oedipa refilled her glass, Metzger had another snort from the bottle. Oedipa then sat five minutes watching the tube, forgetting she was supposed to ask questions. Metzger took his trousers off, earnestly. The father seemed to be up before a court-martial, now.

"So," she said, "an early reel. This is where he gets cashiered, ha, ha."

"Maybe it's a flashback," Metzger said. "Or maybe he gets it twice." Oedipa removed a bracelet. So it went: the succession of film fragments on the tube, the progressive removal of clothing that seemed to bring her no nearer nudity, the boozing, the tireless shivaree of voices and guitars from out by the pool. Now and then a commercial would come in, each time Metzger would say, "Inverarity's," or "Big block of shares," and later settled for nodding and smiling. Oedipa would scowl back, growing more and more certain, while a headache began to flower behind her eyes, that they among all possible combinations of new lovers had found a way to make time itself slow down. Things grew less and less clear. At some point she went into the bathroom, tried to find her image in the mirror and couldn't. She had a moment of nearly pure terror. Then remembered that the mirror had broken and fallen in the sink. "Seven years' bad luck," she said aloud. "I'll be 35." She shut the door behind her and took the occasion to blunder, almost absently, into another slip and skirt, as well as a long-leg girdle and a couple pairs of knee socks. It struck her that if the sun ever came up Metzger would disappear. She wasn't sure if she wanted him to. She came back in to find Metzger wearing only a pair of boxer shorts and fast asleep with a hardon and his head under the couch. She noticed also a fat stomach the suit had hidden. On the screen New Zealanders and Turks were impaling one another on bayonets. With a cry Oedipa rushed to him, fell on him, began kissing him to wake him up. His radiant eyes flew open, pierced her, as if she could feel the sharpness somewhere vague between her breasts. She sank with an enormous sigh that carried all rigidity like a mythical fluid from her, down next to him; so weak she couldn't help him undress her; it took him 20 minutes, rolling, arranging her this way and that, as if she thought, he were some scaled-up, short-haired, poker-faced little girl with a Barbie doll. She may have fallen asleep once or twice. She awoke at last to find herself getting laid; she'd come in on a sexual crescendo in progress, like a cut to a scene where the camera's already moving. Outside a fugue of guitars had begun, and she counted each electronic voice as it came in, till she reached six or so and recalled only three of the Paranoids played guitars; so others must be plugging in.

Which indeed they were. Her climax and Metzger's, when it came, coincided with every light in the place, including the TV tube, suddenly going out, dead, black. It was a curious experience. The Paranoids had blown a fuse. When the lights came on again, and she and Metzger lay twined amid a wall-to-wall scatter of clothing and spilled bourbon, the TV tube revealed the father, dog and Baby Igor trapped inside the darkening "Justine," as the water level inexorably rose. The dog was first to drown, in a great crowd of bubbles. The camera came in for a close-up of Baby Igor crying, one hand on the control board. Something short-circuited then and the grounded Baby Igor was electrocuted, thrashing back and forth and screaming horribly. Through one of those Hollywood distortions in probability, the father was spared electrocution so he could make a farewell speech, apologizing to Baby Igor and the dog for getting them into this and regretting that they wouldn't be meeting in heaven: "Your little eyes have seen your daddy for the last time. You are for salvation; I am for the Pit." At the end his suffering eyes filled the screen, the sound of incoming water grew deafening, up swelled that strange '30's movie music with the massive sax section, in faded the legend THE END.

Oedipa had leaped to her feet and run across to the other wall to turn and glare at Metzger. "They didn't make it!" she yelled. "You bastard, I won."

"You won me," Metzger smiled.

"What did Inverarity tell you about me," she asked finally.

"That you wouldn't be easy."

She began to cry.

"Come back," said Metzger. "Come on."

After awhile she said, "I will." And she did.

3

Things then did not delay in turning curious. If one object behind her discovery of what she was to label the Tristero System or often only The Tristero (as if it might be something's secret title) were to bring to an end her encapsulation in her tower, then that night's infidelity with Metzger would logically be the starting point for it; logically. That's what would come to haunt her most, perhaps: the way it fitted, logically, together. As if (as she'd guessed that first minute in San Narciso) there were revelation in progress all around her.

Much of the revelation was to come through the stamp collection Pierce had left, his substitute often for her—thousands of little colored windows into deep vistas of space and time: savannahs teeming with elands and gazelles, galleons sailing west into the void, Hitler heads, sunsets, cedars of Lebanon, allegorical faces that never were, he could spend hours peering into each one, ignoring her. She had never seen the fascination. The thought that now it would all have to be inventoried and appraised was only another headache. No suspicion at all that it might have something to tell her. Yet if she hadn't been set up or sensitized, first by her peculiar seduction, then by the other, almost offhand things, what after all could the mute stamps have told her, remaining then as they would've only ex-rivals, cheated as she by death, about to be broken up into lots, on route to any number of new masters?

It got seriously under way, this sensitizing, either with the letter from Mucho or the evening she and Metzger drifted into a strange bar known as The Scope. Looking back she forgot which had come first. The letter itself had nothing much to say, had come in response to one of her dutiful, more or less rambling, twice-a-week notes to him, in which she was not confessing to her scene with Metzger because Mucho, she felt, somehow, would know. Would then proceed at a KCUF record hop to look out again across the gleaming gym floor and there in one of the giant keyholes inscribed for basketball see, groping her vertical backstroke a little awkward opposite any boy heels might make her an inch taller than, a Sharon, Linda or Michele, seventeen and what is known as a hip one, whose velveted eyes ultimately, statistically would meet Mucho's and respond, and the thing would develop then groovy as it could when you found you couldn't get statutory rape really out of the back of your law-abiding head. She knew the pattern because it had happened a few times already, though Oedipa had been most scrupulously fair about it, mentioning the practice only once, in fact, another three in the morning and out of a dark dawn sky, asking if he wasn't worried about the penal code. "Of course," said Mucho after awhile, that was all; but in his tone of voice she thought she heard more, something between annoyance and agony. She wondered then if worrying affected his performance. Having once been seventeen and ready to laugh at almost anything, she found herself then overcome by, call it a tenderness she'd never go quite to the back of lest she get bogged. It kept her from asking him any more questions. Like all their inabilities to communicate, this too had a virtuous motive.

It may have been an intuition that the letter would be newsless inside that made Oedipa look more closely at its outside, when it arrived. At first she didn't see. It was an ordinary Muchoesque envelope, swiped from the station, ordinary airmail stamp, to the left of the cancellation a blurb put on by the government, REPORT ALL OBSCENE MAIL TO YOUR POTSMASTER. Idly, she began to skim back through Mucho's letter after reading it to see if there were any dirty words. "Metzger," it occurred to her, "what is a potsmaster?"

"Guy in the scullery," replied Metzger authoritatively from the bathroom, "in charge of all the heavy stuff, canner kettles, gunboats, Dutch ovens . . ."

She threw a brassiere in at him and said, "I'm supposed to report all obscene mail to my potsmaster."

"So they make misprints," Metzger said, "let them. As long as they're careful about not pressing the wrong button, you know?"

It may have been that same evening that they happened across The Scope, a bar out on the way to L.A., near the Yoyodyne plant. Every now and again, like this evening, Echo Courts became impossible, either because of the stillness of the pool and the blank windows that faced on it, or a prevalence of teenage voyeurs, who'd all had copies of Miles's passkey made so they could check in at whim on any bizarre sexual action. This would grow so bad Oedipa and Metzger got in the habit of dragging a mattress into the walk-in closet, where Metzger would then move the chest of drawers up against the door, remove the bottom drawer and put it on top, insert his legs in the empty space, this being the only way he could lie full length in this closet, by which point he'd usually lost interest in the whole thing.

The Scope proved to be a haunt for electronics assembly people from Yoyodyne. The green neon sign outside ingeniously depicted the face of an oscilloscope tube, over which flowed an ever-changing dance of Lissajous figures. Today seemed to be payday, and everyone inside to be drunk already. Glared at all the way, Oedipa and Metzger found a table in back. A wizened bartender wearing shades materialized and Metzger ordered bourbon. Oedipa, checking the bar, grew nervous. There was this je ne sais quoi about the Scope crowd: they all wore glasses and stared at you, silent. Except for a couple-three nearer the door, who were engaged in a nose-picking contest, seeing how far they could flick it across the room.

A sudden chorus of whoops and yibbles burst from a kind of juke box at the far end of the room. Everybody quit talking. The bartender tiptoed back, with the drinks.

"What's happening?" Oedipa whispered.

"That's by Stockhausen," the hip graybeard informed her, "the early crowd tends to dig your Radio Cologne sound. Later on we really swing. We're the only bar in the area, you know, has a strictly electronic music policy. Come on around Saturdays, starting midnight we have your Sinewave Session, that's a live get-together, fellas come in just to jam from all over the state, San Jose, Santa Barbara, San Diego—"

"Live?" Metzger said, "electronic music, live?"

"They put it on the tape, here, live, fella. We got a whole back room full of your audio oscillators, gunshot machines, contact mikes, everything man. That's for if you didn't bring your ax, see, but you got the feeling and you want to swing with the rest of the cats, there's always something available."

"No offense," said Metzger, with a winning Baby Igor smile.

A frail young man in a drip-dry suit slid into the seat across from them, introduced himself as Mike Fallopian, and began proselytizing for an organization known as the Peter Pinguid Society.

"You one of these right-wing nut outfits?" inquired the diplomatic Metzger.

Fallopian twinkled. "They accuse *us* of being paranoids."

"They?" inquired Metzger, twinkling also.

"Us?" asked Oedipa.

The Peter Pinguid Society was named for the commanding officer of the Confederate man-of-war "Disgruntled," who early in 1863 had set sail with the daring plan of bringing a task force around Cape Horn to attack San Francisco and thus open a second front in the War For Southern Independence. Storms and scurvy managed to destroy or discourage every vessel in this armada except the game little "Disgruntled," which showed up off the coast of California about a year later. Unknown, however, to Commodore Pinguid, Czar Nicholas II of Russia had dispatched his Far East Fleet, four corvettes and two clippers, all under the command of one Rear Admiral Popov, to San Francisco Bay, as part of a ploy to keep Britain and France from (among other things) intervening on the side of the Confederacy. Pinguid could not have chosen a worse time for an assault on San Francisco. Rumors were abroad that winter that the Reb cruisers "Alabama" and "Sumter" were indeed on the point of attacking the city, and the Russian admiral had, on his own responsibility, issued his Pacific squadron standing orders to put on steam and clear for action should any such attempt develop. The cruisers, however, seemed to prefer cruising and nothing more. This did not keep Popov from periodic reconnoitering. What happened on the 9th March, 1864, a day now held sacred by all Peter Pinguid Society members, is not too clear. Popov did send out a ship, either the corvette "Bogatir" or the clipper "Gaidamak," to see what it could see. Off the coast of either what is now Carmelby-the-Sea, or what is now Pismo Beach, around noon or possibly toward dusk, the two ships sighted each other. One of them may have fired, if it did then the other responded; but both were out of range so neither showed a scar afterward to prove anything. Night fell. In the morning the Russian ship was gone. But motion is relative. If you believe an excerpt from the "Bogatir" or "Gaidamak" 's log, forwarded in April to the General-Adjutant in St. Petersburg and now somewhere in the Krasnyi Arkhiv, it was the "Disgruntled" that had vanished during the night.

"Who cares?" Fallopian shrugged. "We don't try to make scripture out of it. Naturally that's cost us a lot of support in the Bible Belt, where we might've been expected to go over real good. The old Confederacy.

"But that was the very first military confrontation between Russia and America. Attack, retaliation, both projectiles deep-sixed forever and the Pacific rolls on. But the ripples from those two splashes spread, and grew, and today engulf us all.

"Peter Pinguid was really our first casualty. Not the fanatic our more left-leaning friends over in the Birch Society chose to martyrize."

"Was the Commodore killed, then?" asked Oedipa.

Much worse, to Fallopian's mind. After the confrontation, appalled at what had to be some military alliance between abolitionist Russia (Nicholas having freed the serfs in 1861) and a Union that paid lip-service to abolition while it kept its own industrial laborers in a kind of wage-slavery, Peter Pinguid stayed in his cabin for weeks, brooding.

"But that sounds," objected Metzger, "like he was against industrial capitalism. Wouldn't that disqualify him as any kind of anti-Communist figure?"

"You think like a Bircher," Fallopian said. "Good guys and bad guys. You never get to any of the underlying truth. Sure he was against industrial capitalism. So are we. Didn't it lead, inevitably, to Marxism? Underneath, both are part of the same creeping horror."

"Industrial *anything*," hazarded Metzger.

"There you go," nodded Fallopian.

"What happened to Peter Pinguid?" Oedipa wanted to know.

"He finally resigned his commission. Violated his upbringing and code of honor. Lincoln and the Czar had forced him to. That's what I meant when I said casualty. He and most of the crew settled near L.A.; and for the rest of his life he did little more than acquire wealth."

"How poignant," Oedipa said. "What doing?"

"Speculating in California real estate," said Fallopian. Oedipa, halfway into swallowing part of her drink, sprayed it out again in a glittering cone for ten feet easy, and collapsed in giggles.

"Wha," said Fallopian. "During the drought that year you could've bought lots in the heart of downtown L.A. for 63¢ apiece."

A great shout went up near the doorway, bodies flowed toward a fattish pale young man who'd appeared carrying a leather mailsack over his shoulder.

"Mail call," people were yelling. Sure enough, it was, just like in the army. The fat kid, looking harassed, climbed up on the bar and started calling names and throwing envelopes into the crowd. Fallopian excused himself and joined the others.

Metzger had taken out a pair of glasses and was squinting through them at the kid on the bar. "He's wearing a Yoyodyne badge. What do you make of that?"

"Some inter-office mail run," Oedipa said.

"This time of night?"

"Maybe a late shift?" But Metzger only frowned. "Be back," Oedipa shrugged, heading for the ladies' room.

On the latrine wall, among lipsticked obscenities, she noticed the following message, neatly indited in engineering lettering:

"Interested in sophisticated fun? You, hubby, girl friends. The more the merrier. Get in touch with Kirby, through WASTE only, Box 7391, L. A."

WASTE? Oedipa wondered. Beneath the notice, faintly in pencil, was a symbol she'd never seen before, a loop, triangle and trapezoid, thus:

It might be something sexual, but she somehow doubted it. She found a pen in her purse and copied the address and symbol in her memo book, thinking: God, hieroglyphics. When she came out Fallopian was back, and had this funny look on his face.

"You weren't supposed to see that," he told them. He had an envelope. Oedipa could see, instead of a postage stamp, the handstruck initials PPS.

"Of course," said Metzger. "Delivering the mail is a government monopoly. You would be opposed to that."

Fallopian gave them a wry smile. "It's not as rebellious as it looks. We use Yoyodyne's inter-office delivery. On the sly. But it's hard to find carriers, we have a big turnover. They're run on a tight schedule, and they get nervous. Security people over at the plant know something's up. They keep a sharp eye out. De Witt," pointing at the fat mailman, who was being hauled, twitching, down off the bar and offered drinks he did not want, "he's the most nervous one we've had all year."

"How extensive is this?" asked Metzger.

"Only inside our San Narciso chapter. They've set up pilot projects similar to this in the Washington and I think Dallas chapters. But we're the only one in California so far. A few of your more affluent type members do wrap their letters around bricks, and then the whole thing in brown paper, and send them Railway Express, but I don't know . . ."

"A little like copping out," Metzger sympathized.

"It's the principle," Fallopian agreed, sounding defensive. "To keep it up to some kind of a reasonable volume, each member has to send at least one letter a week through the Yoyodyne system. If you don't, you get fined." He opened his letter and showed Oedipa and Metzger.

Dear Mike, it said, *how are you? Just thought I'd drop you a note. How's your book coming? Guess that's all for now. See you at The Scope.*

"That's how it is," Fallopian confessed bitterly, "most of the time."

"What book did they mean?" asked Oedipa.

Turned out Fallopian was doing a history of private mail delivery in the U. S., attempting to link the Civil War to the postal reform movement that had begun around 1845. He found it beyond simple coincidence that in of all years 1861 the federal government should have set out on a vigorous suppression of those independent mail routes still surviving the various Acts of '45, '47, '51 and '55, Acts all designed to drive any private competition into financial ruin. He saw it all as a parable of power, its feeding, growth and systematic abuse, though he didn't go into it that far with her, that particular night. All Oedipa would remember about him at first, in fact, were his slender build and neat Armenian nose, and a certain affinity of his eyes for green neon.

So began, for Oedipa, the languid, sinister blooming of The

Tristero. Or rather, her attendance at some unique performance, prolonged as if it were the last of the night, something a little extra for whoever'd stayed this late. As if the breakaway gowns, net bras, jeweled garters and G-strings of historical figuration that would fall away were layered dense as Oedipa's own street clothes in that game with Metzger in front of the Baby Igor movie; as if a plunge toward dawn indefinite black hours long would indeed be necessary before The Tristero could be revealed in its terrible nakedness. Would its smile, then, be coy, and would it flirt away harmlessly backstage, say good night with a Bourbon Street bow and leave her in peace? Or would it instead, the dance ended, come back down the runway, its luminous stare locked to Oedipa's, smile gone malign and pitiless; bend to her alone among the desolate rows of seats and begin to speak words she never wanted to hear?

The beginning of that performance was clear enough. It was while she and Metzger were waiting for ancillary letters to be granted representatives in Arizona, Texas, New York and Florida, where Inverarity had developed real estate, and in Delaware, where he'd been incorporated. The two of them, followed by a convertibleful of the Paranoids Miles, Dean, Serge and Leonard and their chicks, had decided to spend the day out at Fangoso Lagoons, one of Inverarity's last big projects. The trip out was uneventful except for two or three collisions the Paranoids almost had owing to Serge, the driver, not being able to see through his hair. He was persuaded to hand over the wheel to one of the girls. Somewhere beyond the battening, urged sweep of three-bedroom houses rushing by their thousands across all the dark beige hills, somehow implicit in an arrogance or bite to the smog the more inland somnolence of San Narciso did lack, lurked the sea, the unimaginable Pacific, the one to which all surfers, beach pads, sewage disposal schemes, tourist incursions, sunned homosexuality, chartered fishing are irrelevant, the hole left by the moon's tearing-free and monument to her exile; you could not hear or even smell this but it was there, something tidal began to reach feelers in past eyes and eardrums, perhaps to arouse fractions of brain current your most gossamer microelectrode is yet too gross for finding. Oedipa had believed, long before leaving Kinneret, in some principle of the sea as redemption for Southern California (not, of course, for her own section of the state, which seemed to need none), some unvoiced idea that no matter what you did to its edges the true Pacific stayed inviolate and integrated or assumed the ugliness at any edge into some more general truth. Perhaps it was only that notion, its arid hope, she sensed as this forenoon they made their seaward thrust, which would stop short of any sea.

They came in among earth-moving machines, a total absence of trees, the usual hieratic geometry, and eventually, shimmying for the sand roads, down in a helix to a sculptured body of water named Lake Inverarity. Out in it, on a round island of fill among blue wavelets, squatted the social hall, a chunky, ogived and verdigrised, Art Nouveau reconstruction of some European pleasure-casino. Oedipa fell in love with it. The Paranoid element piled out of their car, carrying musical instruments and looking around as if for outlets under the trucked-in white sand to plug into. Oedipa from the Impala's trunk took a basket filled with cold eggplant parmigian' sandwiches from an Italian drive-in, and Metzger came up with an enormous Thermos of tequila sours. They wandered all in a loose pattern down the beach toward a small marina for what boat owners didn't have lots directly on the water.

"Hey, blokes," yelled Dean or perhaps Serge, "let's pinch a boat."

"Hear, hear," cried the girls. Metzger closed his eyes and

tripped over an old anchor. "Why are you walking around," inquired Oedipa, "with your eyes closed, Metzger?"

"Larceny," Metzger said, "maybe they'll need a lawyer." A snarl rose along with some smoke from among pleasure boats strung like piglets along the pier, indicating the Paranoids had indeed started someone's outboard. "Come on, then," they called. Suddenly, a dozen boats away, a form, covered with a blue polyethylene tarp, rose up and said, "Baby Igor, I need help."

"I know that voice," said Metzger.

"Quick," said the blue tarp, "let me hitch a ride with you guys."

"Hurry, hurry," called the Paranoids.

"Manny Di Presso," said Metzger, seeming less than delighted.

"Your actor/lawyer friend," Oedipa recalled.

"Not so loud, hey," said Di Presso, skulking as best a polyethylene cone can along the landing towards them. "They're watching. With binoculars." Metzger handed Oedipa aboard the about-to-be-hijacked vessel, a 17-foot aluminum trimaran known as the "Godzilla II," and gave Di Presso what he intended to be a hand also, but he had grabbed, it seemed, only empty plastic, and when he pulled, the entire covering came away and there stood Di Presso, in a skin-diving suit and wraparound shades.

"I can explain," he said.

"Hey," yelled a couple voices, faintly, almost in unison, from up the beach a ways. A squat man with a crew cut, intensely tanned and also with shades, came out in the open running, one arm doubled like a wing with the hand at chest level, inside the jacket.

"Are we on camera?" asked Metzger dryly.

"This is real," chattered Di Presso, "come on." The Paranoids cast off, backed the "Godzilla II" out from the pier, turned and with a concerted whoop took off like a bat out of hell, nearly sending Di Presso over the fantail. Oedipa, looking back, could see their pursuer had been joined by another man about the same build. Both wore gray suits. She couldn't see if they were holding anything like guns.

"I left my car on the other side of the lake," Di Presso said, "but I know he has somebody watching."

"Who does," Metzger asked.

"Anthony Giunghierrace," replied ominous Di Presso, "alias Tony Jaguar."

"Who?"

"Eh, sfacim'," shrugged Di Presso, and spat into their wake. The Paranoids were singing, to the tune of "Adeste Fideles":

Hey, solid citizen, we just pinched your bo-oat,
Hey, solid citizen, we just pinched your boat . . .

grabassing around, trying to push each other over the side. Oedipa cringed out of the way and watched Di Presso. If he had really played the part of Metzger in a TV pilot film as Metzger claimed, the casting had been typically Hollywood: they didn't look or act a bit alike.

"So," said Di Presso, "who's Tony Jaguar. Very big in Cosa Nostra, is who."

"You're an actor," said Metzger. "How are you in with them?"

"I'm a lawyer again," Di Presso said. "That pilot will never be bought, Metz, not unless you go out and do something really Darrowlike, spectacular. Arouse public interest, maybe with a sensational defense."

"Like what."

"Like win the litigation I'm bringing against the estate of Pierce Inverarity." Metzger, as much as cool Metzger could, goggled. Di Presso laughed and punched Metzger in the shoulder. "That's right, good buddy."

"Who wants what? You better talk to the other executor too." He introduced Oedipa, Di Presso tipping his shades politely. The air suddenly went cold, the sun was blotted out. The three looked up in alarm to see looming over them and about to collide the pale green social hall, its towering pointed windows, wrought-iron floral embellishments, solid silence, air somehow of waiting for them. Dean, the Paranoid at the helm, brought the boat around neatly to a small wooden dock, everybody got out, Di Presso heading nervously for an outside staircase. "I want to check on my car," he said. Oedipa and Metzger, carrying picnic stuff, followed up the stairs, along a balcony, out of the building's shadow, up a metal ladder finally to the roof. It was like walking on the head of a drum: they could hear their reverberations inside the hollow building beneath, and the delighted yelling of the Paranoids. Di Presso, Scuba suit glistening, scrambled up the side of a cupola. Oedipa spread a blanket and poured booze into cups made of white, crushed, plastic foam. "It's still there," said Di Presso, descending. "I ought to make a run for it."

"Who's your client?" asked Metzger, holding out a tequila sour.

"Fellow who's chasing me," allowed Di Presso, holding the cup between his teeth so it covered his nose and looking at them, arch.

"You run from clients?" Oedipa asked. "You *flee* ambulances?"

"He's been trying to borrow money," Di Presso said, "since I told him I couldn't get an advance against any settlement in this suit."

"You're all ready to lose, then," she said.

"My heart isn't in it," Di Presso admitted, "and if I can't even keep up payments on that XKE I bought while temporarily insane, how can I lend money?"

"Over 30 years," Metzger snorted, "that's temporary."

"I'm not so crazy I don't know trouble," Di Presso said, "and Tony J. is in it, friends. Gambling mostly, also talk he's been up to show cause to the local Table why he shouldn't be in for some discipline there. That kind of grief I do not need."

Oedipa glared. "You're a selfish schmuck."

"All the time Cosa Nostra is watching," soothed Metzger, "watching. It does not do to be seen helping those the organization does not want helped."

"I have relatives in Sicily," said Di Presso, in comic broken English. Paranoids and their chicks appeared against the bright sky, from behind turrets, gables, ventilating ducts, and moved in on the eggplant sandwiches in the basket. Metzger sat on the jug of booze so they couldn't get any. The wind had risen.

"Tell me about the lawsuit," Metzger said, trying with both hands to keep his hair in place.

"You've been into Inverarity's books," Di Presso said. "You know the Beaconsfield filter thing." Metzger made a noncommittal moue.

"Bone charcoal," Oedipa remembered.

"Yeah, well Tony Jaguar, my client, supplied some bones," said Di Presso, "he alleges. Inverarity never paid him. That's what it's about."

"Offhand," Metzger said, "it doesn't sound like Inverarity. He was scrupulous about payments like that. Unless it was a bribe. I only did his legal tax deductions, so I wouldn't have seen it if it was. What construction firm did your client work for?"

"Construction firm," squinted Di Presso.

Metzger looked around. The Paranoids and their chicks may have been out of earshot. "Human bones, right?" Di Presso nodded yes. "All right, that's how he got them. Different highway outfits in the area, ones Inverarity had bought into, they got the contracts. All drawn up in most kosher fashion, Manfred. If there was payola in there, I doubt it got written down."

"How," inquired Oedipa, "are road builders in any position to sell bones, pray?"

"Old cemeteries have to be ripped up," Metzger explained. "Like in the path of the East San Narciso Freeway, it had no right to be there, so we just barrelled on through, no sweat."

"No bribes, no freeways," Di Presso shaking his head. "These bones came from Italy. A straight sale. Some of them," waving out at the lake, "are down there, to decorate the bottom for the Scuba nuts. That's what I've been doing today, examining the goods in dispute. Till Tony started chasing, anyway. The rest of the bones were used in the R&D phase of the filter program, back around the early '50's, way before cancer. Tony Jaguar says he harvested them all from the bottom of Lago di Pietà."

"My God," Metzger said, soon as this name registered. "GI's?"

"About a company," said Manny Di Presso. Lago di Pietà was near the Tyrrhenian coast, somewhere between Naples and Rome, and had been the scene of a now ignored (in 1943 tragic) battle of attrition in a minor pocket developed during the advance on Rome. For weeks, a handful of American troops, cut off and without communications, huddled on the narrow shore of the clear and tranquil lake while from the cliffs that tilted vertiginously over the beach Germans hit them day and night with plunging, enfilading fire. The water of the lake was too cold to swim: you died of exposure before you could reach any safe shore. There were no trees to build rafts with. No planes came over except an occasional Stuka with strafing in mind. It was remarkable that so few men held out so long. They dug in as far as the rocky beach would let them; they sent small raids up the cliffs that mostly never came back, but did succeed in taking out a machine-gun, once. Patrols looked for routes out, but those few that returned had found nothing. They did what they could to break out; failing, they clung to life as long as they could. But they died, every one, dumbly, without a trace or a word. One day the Germans came down from the cliffs, and their enlisted men put all the bodies that were on the beach into the lake, along with what weapons and other materiel were no longer of use to either side. Presently the bodies sank; and stayed where they were till the early '50's, when Tony Jaguar, who'd been a corporal in an Italian outfit attached to the German force at Lago di Pietà and knew about what was at the bottom, decided along with some colleagues to see what he could salvage. All they managed to come up with was bones. Out of some murky train of reasoning, which may have included the observed fact that American tourists, beginning then to be plentiful, would pay good dollars for almost anything; and stories about Forest Lawn and the American cult of the dead; possibly some dim hope that Senator McCarthy, and others of his persuasion, in those days having achieved a certain ascendancy over the rich cretini from across the sea, would somehow refocus attention on the fallen of WW II, especially ones whose corpses had never been found; out of some such labyrinth of assumed motives, Tony Jaguar decided he could surely unload his harvest of bones on some American someplace, through his contacts in the "family," known these days as Cosa Nostra. He was right. An import-export firm bought the bones, sold them to a fertilizer enterprise, which may have used one or two femurs for laboratory tests but eventually decided to phase entirely into menhaden instead and transferred the remaining several tons to a holding company, which stored them in a warehouse outside of Fort Wayne, Indiana, for maybe a year before Beaconsfield got interested.

"Aha," Metzger leaped. "So it was Beaconsfield bought

them. Not Inverarity. The only shares he held were in Osteolysis, Inc., the company they set up to develop the filter. Never in Beaconsfield itself."

"You know, blokes," remarked one of the girls, a long-waisted, brown-haired lovely in a black knit leotard and pointed sneakers, "this all has a most bizarre resemblance to that ill, ill Jacobean revenge play we went to last week."

"*The Courier's Tragedy*," said Miles, "she's right. The same kind of kinky thing, you know. Bones of lost battalion in lake, fished up, turned into charcoal—"

"They've been listening," screamed Di Presso, "those kids. All the time, somebody listens in, snoops; they bug your apartment, they tap your phone—"

"But we don't repeat what we hear," said another girl. "None of us smoke Beaconsfields anyway. We're all on pot." Laughter. But no joke: for Leonard the drummer now reached into the pocket of his beach robe and produced a fistful of marijuana cigarettes and distributed them among his chums. Metzger closed his eyes, turned his head, muttering, "Possession."

"Help," said Di Presso, looking back with a wild eye and open mouth across the lake. Another runabout had appeared and was headed toward them. Two figures in gray suits crouched behind its windshield. "Metz, I'm running for it. If he stops by here don't bully him, he's my client." And he disappeared down the ladder. Oedipa with a sigh collapsed on her back and stared through the wind at the empty blue sky. Soon she heard the "Godzilla II" starting up.

"Metzger," it occurred to her, "he's taking the boat? We're marooned."

So they were, until well after the sun had set and Miles, Dean, Serge and Leonard and their chicks, by holding up the glowing roaches of their cigarettes like a flipcard section at a football game to spell out alternate S's and O's, attracted the attention of the Fangoso Lagoons Security Force, a garrison against the night made up of one-time cowboy actors and L. A. motorcycle cops. The time in between had been whiled away with songs by the Paranoids, and juicing, and feeding pieces of eggplant sandwich to a flock of not too bright seagulls who'd mistaken Fangoso Langoons for the Pacific, and hearing the plot of *The Courier's Tragedy,* by Richard Wharfinger, related near to unintelligible by eight memories unlooping progressively into regions as strange to map as their rising coils and clouds of pot smoke. It got so confusing that next day Oedipa decided to go see the play itself, and even conned Metzger into taking her.

The Courier's Tragedy was being put on by a San Narciso group known as the Tank Players, the Tank being a small arena theater located out between a traffic analysis firm and a wildcat transistor outfit that hadn't been there last year and wouldn't be this coming but meanwhile was underselling even the Japanese and hauling in loot by the steamshovelful. Oedipa and a reluctant Metzger came in on only a partly-filled house. Attendance did not swell by the time the play started. But the costumes were gorgeous and the lighting imaginative, and though the words were all spoken in Transplanted Middle Western Stage British, Oedipa found herself after five minutes sucked utterly into the landscape of evil Richard Wharfinger had fashioned for his 17th-century audiences, so preapocalyptic, death-wishful, sensually fatigued, unprepared, a little poignantly, for that abyss of civil war that had been waiting, cold and deep, only a few years ahead of them.

Angelo, then, evil Duke of Squamuglia, has perhaps ten years before the play's opening murdered the good Duke of adjoining Faggio, by poisoning the feet on an image of Saint Narcissus, Bishop of Jerusalem, in the court chapel, which feet the Duke was in the habit of kissing every Sunday at Mass. This enables the evil illegitimate son, Pasquale, to take over as regent for his half-brother Niccolò, the rightful heir and good guy of the play, till he comes of age. Pasquale of course has no intention of letting him live so long. Being in thick with the Duke of Squamuglia, Pasquale plots to do away with young Niccolò by suggesting a game of hide-and-seek and then finessing him into crawling inside of an enormous cannon, which a henchman is then to set off, hopefully blowing the child, as Pasquale recalls ruefully, later on in the third act,

> *Out in a bloody rain to feed our fields*
> *Amid the Maenad roar of nitre's song*
> *And sulfur's cantus firmus.*

Ruefully, because the henchman, a likable schemer named Ercole, is secretly involved with dissident elements in the court of Faggio who want to keep Niccolò alive, and so he contrives to stuff a young goat into the cannon instead, meanwhile smuggling Niccolò out of the ducal palace disguised as an elderly procuress.

This comes out in the first scene, as Niccolò confides his history to a friend, Domenico. Niccolò is at this point grown up, hanging around the court of his father's murderer, Duke Angelo, and masquerading as a special courier of the Thurn and Taxis family, who at the time held a postal monopoly throughout most of the Holy Roman Empire. What he is trying to do, ostensibly, is develop a new market, since the evil Duke of Squamuglia has steadfastly refused, even with the lower rates and faster service of the Thurn and Taxis system, to employ any but his own messengers in communicating with his stooge Pasquale over in neighboring Faggio. The real reason Niccolò is waiting around is of course to get a crack at the Duke.

Evil Duke Angelo, meanwhile, is scheming to amalgamate the duchies of Squamuglia and Faggio, by marrying off the only royal female available, his sister Francesca, to Pasquale the Faggian usurper. The only obstacle in the way of this union is that Francesca is Pasquale's mother—her illicit liaison with the good ex-Duke of Faggio being one reason Angelo had him poisoned to begin with. There is an amusing scene where Francesca delicately seeks to remind her brother of the social taboos against incest. They seem to have slipped her mind, replies Angelo, during the ten years he and Francesca have been having *their* affair. Incest or no, the marriage must be; it is vital to his long-range political plans. The Church will never sanction it, says Francesca. So, says Duke Angelo, I will bribe a cardinal. He has begun feeling his sister up and nibbling at her neck; the dialogue modulates into the fevered figures of intemperate desire, and the scene ends with the couple collapsing onto a divan.

The act itself closes with Domenico, to whom the naïve Niccolò started it off by spilling his secret, trying to get in to see Duke Angelo and betray his dear friend. The Duke, of course, is in his apartment busy knocking off a piece, and the best Domenico can do is an administrative assistant who turns out to be the same Ercole who once saved the life of young Niccolò and aided his escape from Faggio. This he presently confesses to Domenico, though only after having enticed that informer into foolishly bending over and putting his head into a curious black box, on the pretext of showing him a pornographic diorama. A steel vise promptly clamps onto the faithless Domenico's head and the box muffles his cries for help. Ercole binds his hands and feet with scarlet silk cords, lets him know who it is he's run afoul of, reaches into the box with a pair of pincers, tears out Domenico's tongue, stabs him a couple times, pours into the box a beaker of aqua regia, enumerates a list of other goodies, including castration, that Domenico will undergo before he's allowed to die, all amid screams, tongueless attempts to pray, agonized struggles from the victim. With the tongue impaled on his rapier Ercole runs to a burning torch set in the wall, sets the tongue aflame and waving it around like a madman concludes the act by screaming,

> *Thy pitiless unmanning is most meet,*
> *Thinks Ercole the zany Paraclete.*
> *Descended this malign, Unholy Ghost,*
> *Let us begin thy frightful Pentecost.*

The lights went out, and in the quiet somebody across the arena from Oedipa distinctly said, "Ick." Metzger said, "You want to go?"

"I want to see about the bones," said Oedipa.

She had to wait till the fourth act. The second was largely spent in the protracted torture and eventual murder of a prince of the church who prefers martyrdom to sanctioning Francesca's marriage to her son. The only interruptions come when Ercole, spying on the cardinal's agony, dispatches couriers to the good-guy element back in Faggio who have it in for Pasquale, telling them to spread the word that Pasquale's planning to marry his mother, calculating this ought to rile up public opinion some; and another scene in which Niccolò, passing the time of day with one of Duke Angelo's couriers, hears the tale of the Lost Guard, a body of some fifty hand-picked knights, the flower of Faggian youth, who once rode as protection for the good Duke. One day, out on manoeuvres near the frontiers of Squamuglia, they all vanished without a trace, and shortly afterward the good Duke got poisoned. Honest Niccolò, who always has difficulty hiding his feelings, observes that if the two events turn out to be at all connected, and can be traced to Duke Angelo, boy, the Duke better watch out, is all. The other courier, one Vittorio, takes offense, vowing in an aside to report this treasonable talk to Angelo at the first opportunity. Meanwhile, back in the torture room, the cardinal is now being forced to bleed into a chalice and consecrate his own blood, not to God, but to Satan. They also cut off his big toe, and he is made to hold it up like a Host and say, "This is my body," the keen-witted Angelo observing that it's the first time he's told anything like the truth in fifty years of systematic lying. Altogether, a most anti-clerical scene, perhaps intended as a sop to the Puritans of the time (a useless gesture since none of them ever went to plays, regarding them for some reason as immoral).

The third act takes place in the court of Faggio, and is spent murdering Pasquale, as the culmination of a coup stirred up by Ercole's agents. While a battle rages in the streets outside the palace, Pasquale is locked up in his patrician hothouse, holding an orgy. Present at the merrymaking is a fierce black performing ape, brought back from a recent voyage to the Indies. Of course it is somebody in an ape suit, who at a signal leaps on Pasquale from a chandelier, at the same time as half a dozen female impersonators who have up to now been lounging around in the guise of dancing girls also move in on the usurper from all parts of the stage. For about ten minutes the vengeful crew proceed to maim, strangle, poison, burn, stomp, blind and otherwise have at Pasquale, while he describes intimately his varied sensations for our enjoyment. He dies finally in extreme agony, and in marches one Gennaro, a complete nonentity, to proclaim himself interim head of state till the rightful Duke, Niccolò, can be located.

There was an intermission. Metzger lurched into the undersized lobby to smoke, Oedipa headed for the ladies' room. She looked idly around for the symbol she'd seen the other night in The Scope, but all the walls, surprisingly, were blank. She could not say why, exactly, but felt threatened by this absence of even the marginal try at communication latrines are known for.

Act IV of *The Courier's Tragedy* discloses evil Duke Angelo in a state of nervous frenzy. He has learned about the coup in

Faggio, the possibility that Niccolò may be alive somewhere after all. Word has reached him that Gennaro is levying a force to invade Squamuglia, also a rumor that the Pope is about to intervene because of the cardinal's murder. Surrounded by treachery on all sides, the Duke has Ercole, whose true role he still does not suspect, finally summon the Thurn and Taxis courier, figuring he can no longer trust his own men. Ercole brings in Niccolò to await the Duke's pleasure. Angelo takes out a quill, parchment and ink, explaining to the audience but not to the good guys, who are still ignorant of recent developments, that to forestall an invasion from Faggio, he must assure Gennaro with all haste of his good intentions. As he scribbles he lets drop a few disordered and cryptic remarks about the ink he's using, implying it's a very special fluid indeed. Like:

> *This pitchy brew in France is "encre" hight;*
> *In this might dire Squamuglia ape the Gaul,*
> *For "anchor" it has ris'n, from deeps untold.*

And:

> *The swan has yielded but one hollow quill,*
> *The hapless mutton, but his tegument;*
> *Yet what, transmuted, swart and silken flows*
> *Between, was neither plucked nor harshly flayed,*
> *But gathered up, from wildly different beasts.*

All of which causes him high amusement. The message to Gennaro completed and sealed, Niccolò tucks it in his doublet and takes off for Faggio, still unaware, as is Ercole, of the coup and his own impending restoration as rightful Duke of Faggio. Scene switches to Gennaro, at the head of a small army, on route to invade Squamuglia. There is a lot of talk to the effect that if Angelo wants peace he'd better send a messenger to let them know before they reach the frontier, otherwise with great reluctance they will hand his ass to him. Back to Squamuglia, where Vittorio, the Duke's courier, reports how Niccolò has been talking treason. Somebody else runs in with news that the body of Domenico, Niccolò's faithless friend, has been found mutilated; but tucked in his shoe was a message, somehow scrawled in blood, revealing Niccolò's true identity. Angelo flies into an apoplectic rage, and orders Niccolò's pursuit and destruction. But not by his own men.

It is at about this point in the play, in fact, that things really get peculiar, and a gentle chill, an ambiguity, begins to creep in among the words. Heretofore the naming of names has gone on either literally or as metaphor. But now, as the Duke gives his fatal command, a new mode of expression takes over. It can only be called a kind of ritual reluctance. Certain things, it is made clear, will not be spoken aloud; certain events will not be shown onstage; though it is difficult to imagine, given the excesses of the preceding acts, what these things could possibly be. The Duke does not, perhaps may not, enlighten us. Screaming at Vittorio he is explicit enough about who shall *not* pursue Niccolò: his own bodyguard he describes to their faces as vermin, zanies, poltroons. But who then will the pursuers be? Vittorio knows: every flunky in the court, idling around in their Squamuglia livery and exchanging Significant Looks, knows. It is all a big in-joke. The audiences of the time knew. Angelo knows, but does not say. As close as he comes does not illuminate:

> *Let him that vizard keep unto his grave,*
> *That vain usurping of an honour'd name;*
> *We'll dance his masque as if it were the truth,*
> *Enlist the poniards swift of Those who, sworn*
> *To punctual vendetta never sleep,*
> *Lest at the palest whisper of the name*

Sweet Niccolò hath stol'n, one trice be lost
In bringing down a fell and soulless doom
Unutterable. . . .

Back to Gennaro and his army. A spy arrives from Squamuglia to tell them Niccolò's on the way. Great rejoicing, in the midst of which Gennaro, who seldom converses, only orates, begs everybody remember that Niccolò is still riding under the Thurn and Taxis colors. The cheering stops. Again, as in Angelo's court, the curious chill creeps in. Everyone onstage (having clearly been directed to do so) becomes aware of a possibility. Gennaro, even less enlightening than Angelo was, invokes the protection of God and Saint Narcissus for Niccolò, and they all ride on. Gennaro asks a lieutenant where they are; turns out it's only a league or so from the lake where Faggio's Lost Guard were last seen before their mysterious disappearance.

Meanwhile, at Angelo's palace, wily Ercole's string has run out at last. Accosted by Vittorio and half a dozen others, he's charged with the murder of Domenico. Witnesses parade in, there is the travesty of a trial, and Ercole meets his end in a refreshingly simple mass stabbing.

We also see Niccolò, in the scene following, for the last time. He has stopped to rest by the shore of a lake where, he remembers being told, the Faggian Guard disappeared. He sits under a tree, opens Angelo's letter, and learns at last of the coup and the death of Pasquale. He realizes that he's riding toward restoration, the love of an entire dukedom, the coming true of all his most virtuous hopes. Leaning against the tree, he reads parts of the letter aloud, commenting, sarcastic, on what is blatantly a pack of lies devised to soothe Gennaro until Angelo can muster his own army of Squamuglians to invade Faggio. Offstage there is a sound of footpads. Niccolò leaps to his feet, staring up one of the radial aisles, hand frozen on the hilt of his sword. He trembles and cannot speak, only stutter, in what may be the shortest line ever written in blank verse: "T-t-t-t . . ." As if breaking out of some dream's paralysis, he begins, each step an effort, to retreat. Suddenly, in lithe and terrible silence, with dancers' grace, three figures, long-limbed, effeminate, dressed in black tights, leotards and gloves, black silk hose pulled over their faces, come capering on stage and stop, gazing at him. Their faces behind the stockings are shadowy and deformed. They wait. The lights all go out.

Back in Squamuglia Angelo is trying to muster an army, without success. Desperate, he assembles those flunkies and pretty girls who are left, ritually locks all his exits, has wine brought in, and begins an orgy.

The act ends with Gennaro's forces drawn up by the shores of the lake. An enlisted man comes on to report that a body, identified as Niccolò by the usual amulet placed round his neck as a child, has been found in a condition too awful to talk about. Again there is silence and everybody looks at everybody else. The soldier hands Gennaro a roll of parchment, stained with blood, which was found on the body. From its seal we can see it's the letter from Angelo that Niccolò was carrying. Gennaro glances at it, does a double-take, reads it aloud. It is no longer the lying document Niccolò read us excerpts from at all, but now miraculously a long confession by Angelo of all his crimes, closing with the revelation of what really happened to the Lost Guard of Faggio. They were—surprise—every one massacred by Angelo and thrown in the lake. Later on their bones were fished up again and made into charcoal, and the charcoal into ink, which Angelo, having a dark sense of humor, used in all his subsequent communications with Faggio, the present document included.

> *But now the bones of these Immaculate*
> *Have mingled with the blood of Niccolò,*
> *And innocence with innocence is join'd,*

A wedlock whose sole child is miracle:
A life's base lie, rewritten into truth.
That truth it is, we all bear testament,
This Guard of Faggio, Faggio's noble dead.

In the presence of the miracle all fall to their knees, bless the
name of God, mourn Niccolò, vow to lay Squamuglia waste. But
Gennaro ends on a note most desperate, probably for its original
audience a real shock, because it names at last the name Angelo
did not and Niccolò tried to:

He that we last as Thurn and Taxis knew
Now recks no lord but the stiletto's Thorn,
And Tacit lies the gold once-knotted horn.
No hallowed skein of stars can ward, I trow,
Who's once been set his tryst with Trystero.

Trystero. The word hung in the air as the act ended and all lights
were for a moment cut; hung in the dark to puzzle Oedipa Maas,
but not yet to exert the power over her it was to.

The fifth act, entirely an anticlimax, is taken up by the blood-
bath Gennaro visits on the court of Squamuglia. Every mode of
violent death available to Renaissance man, including a lye pit,
land mines, a trained falcon with envenom'd talons, is employed.
It plays, as Metzger remarked later, like a Road Runner cartoon
in blank verse. At the end of it about the only character left alive
in a stage dense with corpses is the colorless administrator, Gennaro.

According to the program, *The Courier's Tragedy* had been
directed by one Randolph Driblette. He had also played the part
of Gennaro the winner. "Look, Metzger," Oedipa said, "come on
backstage with me."

"You know one of them?" said Metzger, anxious to leave.

"I want to find out something. I want to talk to Driblette."

"Oh, about the bones." He had a brooding look. Oedipa said,

"I don't know. It just has me uneasy. The two things, so close."

"Fine," Metzger said, "and what next, picket the V.A.? March on Washington? God protect me," he addressed the ceiling of the little theater, causing a few heads among those leaving to swivel, "from these lib, overeducated broads with the soft heads and bleeding hearts. I am 35 years old, and I should know better."

"Metzger," Oedipa whispered, embarrassed, "I'm a Young Republican."

"Hap Harrigan comics," Metzger now even louder, "which she is hardly old enough to read, John Wayne on Saturday afternoon slaughtering ten thousand Japs with his teeth, this is Oedipa Maas's World War II, man. Some people today can drive VW's, carry a Sony radio in their shirt pocket. Not this one, folks, she wants to right wrongs, 20 years after it's all over. Raise ghosts. All from a drunken hassle with Manny Di Presso. Forgetting her first loyalty, legal and moral, is to the estate she represents. Not to our boys in uniform, however gallant, whenever they died."

"It isn't that," she protested. "I don't care what Beaconsfield uses in its filter. I don't care what Pierce bought from the Cosa Nostra. I don't want to think about them. Or about what happened at Lago di Pietà, or cancer . . ." She looked around for words, feeling helpless.

"What then?" Metzger challenged, getting to his feet, looming. "What?"

"I don't know," she said, a little desperate. "Metzger, don't harass me. Be on my side."

"Against whom?" inquired Metzger, putting on shades.

"I want to see if there's a connection. I'm curious."

"Yes, you're curious," Metzger said. "I'll wait in the car, OK?"

Oedipa watched him out of sight, then went looking for dressing rooms; circled the annular corridor outside twice before settling on a door in the shadowy interval between two overhead lights. She walked in on soft, elegant chaos, an impression of emanations, mutually interfering, from the stub-antennas of everybody's exposed nerve endings.

A girl removing fake blood from her face motioned Oedipa on into a region of brightly-lit mirrors. She pushed in, gliding off sweating biceps and momentary curtains of long, swung hair, till at last she stood before Driblette, still wearing his gray Gennaro outfit.

"It was great," said Oedipa.

"Feel," said Driblette, extending his arm. She felt. Gennaro's costume was gray flannel. "You sweat like hell, but nothing else would really be him, right?"

Oedipa nodded. She couldn't stop watching his eyes. They were bright black, surrounded by an incredible network of lines, like a laboratory maze for studying intelligence in tears. They seemed to know what she wanted, even if she didn't.

"You came to talk about the play," he said. "Let me discourage you. It was written to entertain people. Like horror movies. It isn't literature, it doesn't mean anything. Wharfinger was no Shakespeare."

"Who was he?" she said.

"Who was Shakespeare. It was a long time ago."

"Could I see a script?" She didn't know what she was looking for, exactly. Driblette motioned her over to a file cabinet next to the one shower.

"I'd better grab a shower," he said, "before the Drop-The-Soap crowd get here. Scripts're in the top drawer."

But they were all purple, Dittoed—worn, torn, stained with coffee. Nothing else in the drawer. "Hey," she yelled into the shower. "Where's the original? What did you make these copies from?"

"A paperback," Driblette yelled back. "Don't ask me the publisher. I found it at Zapf's Used Books over by the freeway. It's an anthology, *Jacobean Revenge Plays*. There was a skull on the cover."

"Could I borrow it?"

"Somebody took it. Opening night parties. I lose at least half a dozen every time." He stuck his head out of the shower. The rest of his body was wreathed in steam, giving his head an eerie, balloon-like buoyancy. Careful, staring at her with deep amusement, he said, "There was another copy there. Zapf might still have it. Can you find the place?"

Something came to her viscera, danced briefly, and went. "Are you putting me on?" For awhile the furrowed eyes only gazed back.

"Why," Driblette said at last, "is everybody so interested in texts?"

"Who else?" Too quickly. Maybe he had only been talking in general.

Driblette's head wagged back and forth. "Don't drag me into your scholarly disputes," adding "whoever you all are," with a familiar smile. Oedipa realized then, cold corpse-fingers of grue on her skin, that it was exactly the same look he'd coached his cast to give each other whenever the subject of the Trystero assassins came up. The knowing look you get in your dreams from a certain unpleasant figure. She decided to ask about this look.

"Was it written in as a stage direction? All those people, so obviously in on something. Or was that one of your touches?"

"That was my own," Driblette told her, "that, and actually bringing the three assassins onstage in the fourth act. Wharfinger didn't show them at all, you know."

"Why did you? Had you heard about them somewhere else?"

"You don't understand," getting mad. "You guys, you're like Puritans are about the Bible. So hung up with words, words. You know where that play exists, not in that file cabinet, not in any paperback you're looking for, but—" a hand emerged from the veil of shower-steam to indicate his suspended head—"in here. That's what I'm for. To give the spirit flesh. The words, who cares? They're rote noises to hold line bashes with, to get past the bone barriers around an actor's memory, right? But the reality is in *this* head. Mine. I'm the projector at the planetarium, all the closed little universe visible in the circle of that stage is coming out of my mouth, eyes, sometimes other orifices also."

But she couldn't let it quite go. "What made you feel differently than Wharfinger did about this, this Trystero." At the word, Driblette's face abruptly vanished, back into the steam. As if switched off. Oedipa hadn't wanted to say the word. He had managed to create around it the same aura of ritual reluctance here, offstage, as he had on.

"If I were to dissolve in here," speculated the voice out of the drifting steam, "be washed down the drain into the Pacific, what you saw tonight would vanish too. You, that part of you so concerned, God knows how, with that little world, would also vanish. The only residue in fact would be things Wharfinger didn't lie about. Perhaps Squamuglia and Faggio, if they ever existed. Perhaps the Thurn and Taxis mail system. Stamp collectors tell me it did exist. Perhaps the other, also. The Adversary. But they would be traces, fossils. Dead, mineral, without value or potential.

"You could fall in love with me, you can talk to my shrink, you can hide a tape recorder in my bedroom, see what I talk about from wherever I am when I sleep. You want to do that? You can put together clues, develop a thesis, or several, about why characters reacted to the Trystero possibility the way they did, why the assassins came on, why the black costumes. You could waste your life that way and never touch the truth. Wharfinger supplied words and a yarn. I gave them life. That's it." He fell silent. The shower splashed.

"Driblette?" Oedipa called, after awhile.

His face appeared briefly. "We could do that." He wasn't smiling. His eyes waited, at the centers of their webs.

"I'll call," said Oedipa. She left, and was all the way outside before thinking, I went in there to ask about bones and instead we talked about the Trystero thing. She stood in a nearly deserted parking lot, watching the headlights of Metzger's car come at her, and wondered how accidental it had been.

Metzger had been listening to the car radio. She got in and rode with him for two miles before realizing that the whimsies of nighttime reception were bringing them KCUF down from Kinneret, and that the disk jockey talking was her husband, Mucho.

4

Though she saw Mike Fallopian again, and did trace the text of The
Courier's Tragedy *a certain distance*, these follow-ups were no
more disquieting than other revelations which now seemed to
come crowding in exponentially, as if the more she collected the
more would come to her, until everything she saw, smelled,
dreamed, remembered, would somehow come to be woven into
The Tristero.

For one thing, she read over the will more closely. If it was
really Pierce's attempt to leave an organized something behind
after his own annihilation, then it was part of her duty, wasn't it,
to bestow life on what had persisted, to try to be what Driblette
was, the dark machine in the center of the planetarium, to bring
the estate into pulsing stelliferous Meaning, all in a soaring dome
around her? If only so much didn't stand in her way: her deep
ignorance of law, of investment, of real estate, ultimately of the
dead man himself. The bond the probate court had had her post
was perhaps their evaluation in dollars of how much did stand in
her way. Under the symbol she'd copied off the latrine wall of
The Scope into her memo book, she wrote *Shall I project a world?*

If not project then at least flash some arrow on the dome to skitter among constellations and trace out your Dragon, Whale, Southern Cross. Anything might help.

It was some such feeling that got her up early one morning to go to a Yoyodyne stockholders' meeting. There was nothing she could do at it, yet she felt it might redeem her a little from inertia. They gave her a round white visitor's badge at one of the gates, and she parked in an enormous lot next to a quonset building painted pink and about a hundred yards long. This was the Yoyodyne Cafeteria, and scene of her meeting. For two hours Oedipa sat on a long bench between old men who might have been twins and whose hands, alternately (as if their owners were asleep and the moled, freckled hands out roaming dream-landscapes) kept falling onto her thighs. Around them all, Negroes carried gunboats of mashed potatoes, spinach, shrimp, zucchini, pot roast, to the long, glittering steam tables, preparing to feed a noontide invasion of Yoyodyne workers. The routine business took an hour; for another hour the shareholders and proxies and company officers held a Yoyodyne songfest. To the tune of Cornell's alma mater, they sang:

HYMN

> *High above the L. A. freeways,*
> *And the traffic's whine,*
> *Stands the well-known Galactronics*
> *Branch of Yoyodyne.*
> *To the end, we swear undying*
> *Loyalty to you,*
> *Pink pavilions bravely shining,*
> *Palm trees tall and true.*

Being led in this by the president of the company, Mr. Clayton ("Bloody") Chiclitz himself; and to the tune of "Aura Lee":

GLEE

Bendix guides the warheads in,
Avco builds them nice.
Douglas, North American,
Grumman get their slice.
Martin launches off a pad,
Lockheed from a sub;
We can't get the R&D
On a Piper Cub.
Convair boosts the satellite
Into orbits round;
Boeing builds the Minuteman,
We stay on the ground.
Yoyodyne, Yoyodyne,
Contracts flee thee yet.
DOD has shafted thee,
Out of spite, I'll bet.

And dozens of other old favorites whose lyrics she couldn't remember. The singers were then formed into platoon-sized groups for a quick tour of the plant.

Somehow Oedipa got lost. One minute she was gazing at a mockup of a space capsule, safely surrounded by old, somnolent men; the next, alone in a great, fluorescent murmur of office activity. As far as she could see in any direction it was white or pastel: men's shirts, papers, drawing boards. All she could think of was to put on her shades for all this light, and wait for somebody to rescue her. But nobody noticed. She began to wander aisles among light blue desks, turning a corner now and then. Heads came up at the sound of her heels, engineers stared until she'd passed, but nobody spoke to her. Five or ten minutes went by this way, panic growing inside her head: there seemed no way out of the area. Then, by accident (Dr. Hilarius, if asked, would accuse her of using subliminal cues in the environment to guide her to a particular person) or howsoever, she came on one Stanley Koteks, who wore wire-rim bifocals, sandals, argyle socks, and at first glance seemed too young to be working here. As it turned out he wasn't working, only doodling with a fat felt pencil this sign: ⊙

"Hello there," Oedipa said, arrested by this coincidence. On a whim, she added, "Kirby sent me," this having been the name on the latrine wall. It was supposed to sound conspiratorial, but came out silly.

"Hi," said Stanley Koteks, deftly sliding the big envelope he'd been doodling on into an open drawer he then closed. Catching sight of her badge, "You're lost, huh?"

She knew blunt questions like, what does that symbol mean? would get her nowhere. She said, "I'm a tourist, actually. A stockholder."

"Stockholder." He gave her the once-over, hooked with his foot a swivel chair from the next desk and rolled it over for her. "Sit down. Can you really influence policy, or make suggestions they won't just file in the garbage?"

"Yes," lied Oedipa, to see where it would take them.

"See," Koteks said, "if you can get them to drop their clause on patents. That, lady, is my ax to grind."

"Patents," Oedipa said. Koteks explained how every engineer, in signing the Yoyodyne contract, also signed away the patent rights to any inventions he might come up with.

"This stifles your really creative engineer," Koteks said, adding bitterly, "wherever he may be."

"I didn't think people invented any more," said Oedipa, sensing this would goad him. "I mean, who's there been, really, since Thomas Edison? Isn't it all teamwork now?" Bloody Chiclitz, in his welcoming speech this morning, had stressed teamwork.

"Teamwork," Koteks snarled, "is one word for it, yeah. What it really is is a way to avoid responsibility. It's a symptom of the gutlessness of the whole society."

"Goodness," said Oedipa, "are you allowed to talk like that?"

Koteks looked to both sides, then rolled his chair closer. "You know the Nefastis Machine?" Oedipa only widened her eyes. "Well this was invented by John Nefastis, who's up at Berkeley now. John's somebody who still invents things. Here. I have a copy of the patent." From a drawer he produced a Xeroxed wad of papers, showing a box with a sketch of a bearded Victorian on its outside, and coming out of the top two pistons attached to a crankshaft and flywheel.

"Who's that with the beard?" asked Oedipa. James Clerk Maxwell, explained Koteks, a famous Scotch scientist who had once postulated a tiny intelligence, known as Maxwell's Demon. The Demon could sit in a box among air molecules that were moving at all different random speeds, and sort out the fast molecules from the slow ones. Fast molecules have more energy than slow ones. Concentrate enough of them in one place and you have a region of high temperature. You can then use the difference in temperature between this hot region of the box and any cooler region, to drive a heat engine. Since the Demon only sat and sorted, you wouldn't have put any real work into the system. So you would be violating the Second Law of Thermodynamics, getting something for nothing, causing perpetual motion.

"Sorting isn't work?" Oedipa said. "Tell them down at the post office, you'll find yourself in a mailbag headed for Fairbanks, Alaska, without even a FRAGILE sticker going for you."

"It's mental work," Koteks said, "But not work in the thermodynamic sense." He went on to tell how the Nefastis Machine contained an honest-to-God Maxwell's Demon. All you had to do was stare at the photo of Clerk Maxwell, and concentrate on which cylinder, right or left, you wanted the Demon to raise the temperature in. The air would expand and push a piston. The familiar Society for the Propagation of Christian Knowledge photo, showing Maxwell in right profile, seemed to work best.

Oedipa, behind her shades, looked around carefully, trying not to move her head. Nobody paid any attention to them: the air-conditioning hummed on, IBM typewriters chiggered away, swivel chairs squeaked, fat reference manuals were slammed shut, rattling blueprints folded and refolded, while high overhead the long silent fluorescent bulbs glared merrily; all with Yoyodyne was normal. Except right here, where Oedipa Maas, with a thousand other people to choose from, had had to walk uncoerced into the presence of madness.

"Not everybody can work it, of course," Koteks, having warmed to his subject, was telling her. "Only people with the gift. 'Sensitives,' John calls them."

Oedipa rested her shades on her nose and batted her eyelashes, figuring to coquette her way off this conversational hook: "Would I make a good sensitive, do think?"

"You really want to try it? You could write to him. He only knows a few sensitives. He'd let you try."

Oedipa took out her little memo book and opened to the symbol she'd copied and the words *Shall I project a world?* "Box 573," said Koteks.

"In Berkeley."

"No," his voice gone funny, so that she looked up, too sharply, by which time, carried by a certain momentum of thought, he'd also said, "In San Francisco; there's none——" and by then knew he'd made a mistake. "He's living somewhere along Telegraph," he muttered. "I gave you the wrong address."

She took a chance: "Then the WASTE address isn't good any more." But she'd pronounced it like a word, waste. His face congealed, a mask of distrust. "It's W.A.S.T.E., lady," he told her, "an acronym, not 'waste,' and we had best not go into it any further."

"I saw it in a ladies' john," she confessed. But Stanley Koteks was no longer about to be sweettalked.

"Forget it," he advised; opened a book and proceeded to ignore her.

She in her turn, clearly, was not about to forget it. The envelope she'd seen Koteks doodling what she'd begun to think of as the "WASTE symbol" on had come, she bet, from John Nefastis. Or somebody like him. Her suspicions got embellished by, of all people, Mike Fallopian of the Peter Pinguid Society.

"Sure this Koteks is part of some underground," he told her a few days later, "an underground of the unbalanced, possibly, but then how can you blame them for being maybe a little bitter? Look what's happening to them. In school they got brainwashed, like all of us, into believing the Myth of the American Inventor—Morse and his telegraph, Bell and his telephone, Edison and his light bulb, Tom Swift and his this or that. Only one man per invention. Then when they grew up they found they had to sign over all their rights to a monster like Yoyodyne; got stuck on some 'project' or 'task force' or 'team' and started being ground into anonymity. Nobody wanted them to invent—only perform their little role in a design ritual, already set down for them in some procedures handbook. What's it like, Oedipa, being all alone in a nightmare like that? Of course they stick together, they keep in touch. They can always tell when they come on another of their kind. Maybe it only happens once every five years, but still, immediately, they know."

Metzger, who'd come along to The Scope that evening, wanted to argue. "You're so right-wing you're left-wing," he protested. "How can you be against a corporation that wants a worker to waive his patent rights. That sounds like the surplus value theory to me, fella, and you sound like a Marxist." As they got drunker this typical Southern California dialogue degenerated further. Oedipa sat alone and gloomy. She'd decided to come tonight to The Scope not only because of the encounter with Stanley Koteks, but also because of other revelations; because it seemed that a pattern was beginning to emerge, having to do with the mail and how it was delivered.

There had been the bronze historical marker on the other side of the lake at Fangoso Lagoons. *On this site,* it read, *in 1853, a dozen Wells, Fargo men battled gallantly with a band of masked marauders in mysterious black uniforms. We owe this description to a post rider, the only witness to the massacre, who died shortly after. The only other clue was a cross, traced by one of the victims in the dust. To this day the identities of the slayers remain shrouded in mystery.*

A cross? Or the initial T? The same stuttered by Niccolò in *The Courier's Tragedy.* Oedipa pondered this. She called Randolph Driblette from a pay booth, to see it he'd known about this Wells, Fargo incident; if that was why he'd chosen to dress his bravos all in black. The phone buzzed on and on, into hollowness. She hung up and headed for Zapf's Used Books. Zapf himself came forward out of a wan cone of 15-watt illumination to help her find the paperback Driblette had mentioned, *Jacobean Revenge Plays.*

"It's been very much in demand," Zapf told her. The skull on the cover watched them, through the dim light.

Did he only mean Driblette? She opened her mouth to ask, but didn't. It was to be the first of many demurs.

Back at Echo Courts, Metzger in L.A. for the day on other business, she turned immediately to the single mention of the word Trystero. Opposite the line she read, in pencil, *Cf. variant, 1687 ed.* Put there maybe by some student. In a way, it cheered her. Another reading of that line might help light further the dark face of the word. According to a short preface, the text had been taken from a folio edition, undated. Oddly, the preface was unsigned. She checked the copyright page and found that the original hardcover had been a textbook, *Plays of Ford, Webster, Tourneur and Wharfinger*, published by The Lectern Press, Berkeley, California, back in 1957. She poured herself half a tumbler of Jack Daniels (the Paranoids having left them a fresh bottle the evening before) and called the L.A. library. They checked, but didn't have the hardcover. They could look it up on inter-library loan for her. "Wait," she said, having just got an idea, "the publisher's up in Berkeley. Maybe I'll try them directly." Thinking also that she could visit John Nefastis.

She had caught sight of the historical marker only because she'd gone back, deliberately, to Lake Inverarity one day, owing to this, what you might have to call, growing obsession, with "bringing something of herself"—even if that something was just her presence—to the scatter of business interests that had survived Inverarity. She would give them order, she would create constellations; next day she drove out to Vesperhaven House, a home for senior citizens that Inverarity had put up around the time Yoyodyne came to San Narciso. In its front recreation room she found sunlight coming in it seemed through every window; an old man nodding in front of a dim Leon Schlesinger cartoon show on the tube; and a black fly browsing along the pink, dandruffy arroyo of the neat part in the old man's hair. A fat nurse ran in with a can of bug spray and yelled at the fly to take off so she could kill it. The cagy fly stayed where it was. "You're bothering Mr Thoth," she yelled at the little fellow. Mr Thoth jerked awake, jarring loose the fly, which made a desperate scramble for the door. The nurse pursued, spraying poison.

"Hello," said Oedipa.

"I was dreaming," Mr Thoth told her, "about my grandfather. A very old man, at least as old as I am now, 91. I thought, when I was a boy, that he had been 91 all his life. Now I feel," laughing, "as if *I* have been 91 all my life. Oh, the stories that old man would tell. He rode for the Pony Express, back in the gold rush days. His horse was named Adolf, I remember that."

Oedipa, sensitized, thinking of the bronze marker, smiled at him as granddaughterly as she knew how and asked, "Did he ever have to fight off desperados?"

"That cruel old man," said Mr Thoth, "was an Indian killer. God, the saliva would come out in a string from his lip whenever he told about killing the Indians. He must have loved that part of it."

"What were you dreaming about him?"

"Oh, that," perhaps embarrassed. "It was all mixed in with a Porky Pig cartoon." He waved at the tube. "It comes into your dreams, you know. Filthy machine. Did you ever see the one about Porky Pig and the anarchist?"

She had, as a matter of fact, but she said no.

"The anarchist is dressed all in black. In the dark you can only see his eyes. It dates from the 1930's. Porky Pig is a little boy. The children told me that he has a nephew now, Cicero. Do you remember, during the war, when Porky worked in a defense plant? He and Bugs Bunny. That was a good one too."

"Dressed all in black," Oedipa prompted him.

"It was mixed in so with the Indians," he tried to remember, "the dream. The Indians who wore black feathers, the Indians who weren't Indians. My grandfather told me. The feathers were white, but those false Indians were supposed to burn bones and stir the boneblack with their feathers to get them black. It made them invisible in the night, because they came at night. That was how the old man, bless him, knew they weren't Indians. No

Indian ever attacked at night. If he got killed his soul would wander in the dark forever. Heathen."

"If they weren't Indians," Oedipa asked, "what were they?"

"A Spanish name," Mr Thoth said, frowning, "a Mexican name. Oh, I can't remember. Did they write it on the ring?" He reached down to a knitting bag by his chair and came up with blue yarn, needles, patterns, finally a dull gold signet ring. "My grandfather cut this from the finger of one of them he killed. Can you imagine a 91-year-old man so brutal?" Oedipa stared. The device on the ring was once again the WASTE symbol.

She looked around, spooked at the sunlight pouring in all the windows, as if she had been trapped at the center of some intricate crystal, and said, "My God."

"And I feel him, certain days, days of a certain temperature," said Mr Thoth, "and barometric pressure. Did you know that? I feel him close to me."

"Your grandfather?"

"No, my God."

So she went to find Fallopian, who ought to know a lot about the Pony Express and Wells, Fargo if he was writing a book about them. He did, but not about their dark adversaries.

"I've had hints," he told her, "sure. I wrote to Sacramento about that historical marker, and they've been kicking it around their bureaucratic morass for months. Someday they'll come back with a source book for me to read. It will say, 'Old-timers remember the yarn about,' whatever happened. Old-timers. Real good documentation, this Californiana crap. Odds are the author will be dead. There's no way to trace it, unless you want to follow up an accidental correlation, like you got from the old man."

"You think it's really a correlation?" She thought of how tenuous it was, like a long white hair, over a century long. Two very old men. All these fatigued brain cells between herself and the truth.

"Marauders, nameless, faceless, dressed in black. Probably hired by the Federal government. Those suppressions were brutal."

"Couldn't it have been a rival carrier?"

Fallopian shrugged. Oedipa showed him the WASTE symbol, and he shrugged again.

"It was in the ladies' room, right here in The Scope, Mike."

"Women," he only said. "Who can tell what goes on with them?"

If she'd thought to check a couple lines back in the Wharfinger play, Oedipa might have made the next connection by herself. As it was she got an assist from one Genghis Cohen, who is the most eminent philatelist in the L.A. area. Metzger, acting on instructions in the will, had retained this amiable, slightly adenoidal expert, for a percent of his valuation, to inventory and appraise Inverarity's stamp collection.

One rainy morning, with mist rising off the pool, Metzger again away, the Paranoids off somewhere to a recording session, Oedipa got rung up by this Genghis Cohen, who even over the phone she could tell was disturbed.

"There are some irregularities, Miz Maas," he said. "Could you come over?"

She was somehow sure, driving in on the slick freeway, that the "irregularities" would tie in with the word Trystero. Metzger had taken the stamp albums to Cohen from safe-deposit storage a week ago in Oedipa's Impala, and then she hadn't even been interested enough to look inside them. But now it came to her, as if the rain whispered it, that what Fallopian had not known about private carriers, Cohen might.

When he opened the door of his apartment/office she saw him framed in a long succession or train of doorways, room after room receding in the general direction of Santa Monica, all soaked in rain-light. Genghis Cohen had a touch of summer flu, his fly was half open and he was wearing a Barry Goldwater sweatshirt also. Oedipa felt at once motherly. In a room perhaps a third of the way along the suite he sat her in a rocking chair and brought real homemade dandelion wine in small neat glasses.

"I picked the dandelions in a cemetery, two years ago. Now the cemetery is gone. They took it out for the East San Narciso Freeway."

She could, at this stage of things, recognize signals like that, as the epileptic is said to—an odor, color, pure piercing grace note announcing his seizure. Afterward it is only this signal, really dross, this secular announcement, and never what is revealed during the attack, that he remembers. Oedipa wondered whether, at the end of this (if it were supposed to end), she too might not be left with only compiled memories of clues, announcements, intimations, but never the central truth itself, which must somehow each time be too bright for her memory to hold; which must always blaze out, destroying its own message irreversibly, leaving an overexposed blank when the ordinary world came back. In the space of a sip of dandelion wine it came to her that she would never know how many times such a seizure may already have visited, or how to grasp it should it visit again. Perhaps even in this last second—but there was no way to tell. She glanced down the corridor of Cohen's rooms in the rain and saw, for the very first time, how far it might be possible to get lost in this.

"I have taken the liberty," Genghis Cohen was saying, "of getting in touch with an Expert Committee. I haven't yet forwarded them the stamps in question, pending your own authorization and of course Mr. Metzger's. However, all fees, I am sure, can be charged to the estate."

"I'm not sure I understand," Oedipa said.

"Allow me." He rolled over to her a small table, and from a

plastic folder lifted with tweezers, delicately, a U. S. commemorative stamp, the Pony Express issue of 1940, 3¢ henna brown. Cancelled. "Look," he said, switching on a small, intense lamp, handing her an oblong magnifying glass.

"It's the wrong side," she said, as he swabbed the stamp gently with benzine and placed it on a black tray.

"The watermark."

Oedipa peered. There it was again, her WASTE symbol, showing up black, a little right of center.

"What is this?" she asked, wondering how much time had gone by.

"I'm not sure," Cohen said. "That's why I've referred it, and the others, to the Committee. Some friends have been around to see them too, but they're all being cautious. But see what you think of this." From the same plastic folder he now tweezed what looked like an old German stamp, with the figures ¼ in the centre, the word *Freimarke* at the top, and along the right-hand margin the legend *Thurn und Taxis*.

"They were," she remembered from the Wharfinger play, "some kind of private couriers, right?"

"From about 1300, until Bismarck bought them out in 1867, Miz Maas, they were *the* European mail service. This is one of their very few adhesive stamps. But look in the corners." Decorating each corner of the stamp, Oedipa saw a horn with a single loop in it. Almost like the WASTE symbol. "A post horn," Cohen said; "the Thurn and Taxis symbol. It was in their coat of arms."

And Tacit lies the gold once-knotted horn, Oedipa remembered. Sure. "Then the watermark you found," she said, "is nearly the same thing, except for the extra little doojigger sort of coming out of the bell."

"It sounds ridiculous," Cohen said, "but my guess is it's a mute."

She nodded. The black costumes, the silence, the secrecy. Whoever they were their aim was to mute the Thurn and Taxis post horn.

"Normally this issue, and the others, are unwatermarked," Cohen said, "and in view of other details—the hatching, number of perforations, way the paper has aged—it's obviously a counterfeit. Not just an error."

"Then it isn't worth anything."

Cohen smiled, blew his nose. "You'd be amazed how much you can sell an honest forgery for. Some collectors specialize in them. The question is, who did these? They're atrocious." He flipped the stamp over and with the tip of the tweezers showed her. The picture had a Pony Express rider galloping out of a western fort. From shrubbery over on the right-hand side and possibly in the direction the rider would be heading, protruded a single, painstakingly engraved, black feather. "Why put in a deliberate mistake?" he asked, ignoring—if he saw it—the look on her face. "I've come up so far with eight in all. Each one has an error like this, laboriously worked into the design, like a taunt. There's even a transposition—U. S. *Potsage,* of all things."

"How recent?" blurted Oedipa, louder than she needed to be.

"Is anything wrong, Miz Maas?"

She told him first about the letter from Mucho with a cancellation telling her report all obscene mail to her potsmaster.

"Odd," Cohen agreed. "The transposition," consulting a notebook, "is only on the Lincoln 4¢. Regular issue, 1954. The other forgeries run back to 1893."

"That's 70 years," she said. "He'd have to be pretty old."

"If it's the same one," said Cohen. "And what if it were as old as Thurn and Taxis? Omedio Tassis, banished from Milan, organized his first couriers in the Bergamo region around 1290."

They sat in silence, listening to rain gnaw languidly at the windows and skylights, confronted all at once by the marvellous possibility.

"Has that ever happened before?" she had to ask.

"An 800-year tradition of postal fraud. Not to my knowledge." Oedipa told him then all about old Mr Thoth's signet ring, and the symbol she'd caught Stanley Koteks doodling, and the muted horn drawn in the ladies' room at The Scope.

"Whatever it is," he hardly needed to say, "they're apparently still quite active."

"Do we tell the government, or what?"

"I'm sure they know more than we do." He sounded nervous, or suddenly in retreat. "No, I wouldn't. It isn't our business, is it?"

She asked him then about the initials W.A.S.T.E., but it was somehow too late. She'd lost him. He said no, but so abruptly out of phase now with her own thoughts he could even have been lying. He poured her more dandelion wine.

"It's clearer now," he said, rather formal. "A few months ago it got quite cloudy. You see, in spring, when the dandelions begin to bloom again, the wine goes through a fermentation. As if they remembered."

No, thought Oedipa, sad. As if their home cemetery in some way still did exist, in a land where you could somehow walk, and not need the East San Narciso Freeway, and bones still could rest in peace, nourishing ghosts of dandelions, no one to plow them up. As if the dead really do persist, even in a bottle of wine.

5

Though her next move should have been to contact Randolph Driblette again, she decided instead to drive up to Berkeley. She wanted to find out where Richard Wharfinger had got his information about Trystero. Possibly also take a look at how the inventor John Nefastis picked up his mail.

As with Mucho when she'd left Kinneret, Metzger did not seem desperate at her going. She debated, driving north, whether to stop off at home on the way to Berkeley or coming back. As it turned out she missed the exit for Kinneret and that solved it. She purred along up the east side of the bay, presently climbed into the Berkeley hills and arrived close to midnight at a sprawling, many-leveled, German-baroque hotel, carpeted in deep green, going in for curved corridors and ornamental chandeliers. A sign in the lobby said WELCOME CALIFORNIA CHAPTER AMERICAN DEAF-MUTE ASSEMBLY. Every light in the place burned, alarmingly bright; a truly ponderable silence occupied the building. A clerk popped up from behind the desk where he'd been sleeping and began making sign language at her. Oedipa considered giving him the finger to see what would happen. But she'd driven straight through, and all at once the fatigue of it had caught up with her. The clerk took her to a room with a reproduction of a Remedios Varo in it, through corridors gently curving as the streets of San Narciso, utterly silent. She fell asleep almost at once, but kept waking from a nightmare about something in the mirror, across from her bed. Nothing specific, only a possibility, nothing she could see. When she finally did settle into sleep, she dreamed that Mucho, her husband, was making love to her on a soft white beach that was not part of any California she knew. When she woke in the morning, she was sitting bolt upright, staring into the mirror at her own exhausted face.

She found the Lectern Press in a small office building on Shattuck Avenue. They didn't have *Plays of Ford, Webster, Tourneur and Wharfinger* on the premises, but did take her check for $12.50, gave her the address of their warehouse in Oakland and a receipt to show the people there. By the time she'd collected the book, it was afternoon. She skimmed through to find the line that had brought her all the way up here. And in the leaf-fractured sunlight, froze.

No hallowed skein of stars can ward, I trow, ran the couplet, *Who once has crossed the lusts of Angelo.*

"No," she protested aloud. " 'Who's once been set his tryst with Trystero.' " The pencilled note in the paperback had mentioned a variant. But the paperback was supposed to be a straight reprint of the book she now held. Puzzled, she saw that this edition also had a footnote:

> According only to the Quarto edition (1687). The earlier Folio has a lead inserted where the closing line should have been. D'Amico has suggested that Wharfinger may have made a libellous comparison involving someone at court, and that the later 'restoration' was actually the work of the printer, Inigo Barfstable. The doubtful 'Whitechapel' version

(c. 1670) has 'This tryst or odious awry, O Niccolò,' which besides bringing in a quite graceless Alexandrine, is difficult to make sense of syntactically, unless we accept the rather unorthodox though persuasive argument of J.-K. Sale that the line is really a pun on 'This trystero *dies irae.* . . .' This, however, it must be pointed out, leaves the line nearly as corrupt as before, owing to no clear meaning for the word *trystero,* unless it be a pseudo-Italianate variant on *triste* (= wretched, depraved). But the 'Whitechapel' edition, besides being a fragment, abounds in such corrupt and probably spurious lines, as we have mentioned elsewhere, and is hardly to be trusted.

Then where, Oedipa wondered, does the paperback I bought at Zapf's get off with *its* "Trystero" line? Was there yet another edition, besides the Quarto, Folio, and "Whitechapel" fragment? The editor's preface, signed this time, by one Emory Bortz, professor of English at Cal, mentioned none. She spent nearly an hour more, searching through all the footnotes, finding nothing.

"Dammit," she yelled, started the car and headed for the Berkeley campus, to find Professor Bortz.

She should have remembered the date on the book—1957. Another world. The girl in the English office informed Oedipa that Professor Bortz was no longer with the faculty. He was teaching at San Narciso College, San Narciso, California.

Of course, Odeipa thought, wry, where else? She copied the address and walked away trying to remember who'd put out the paperback. She couldn't.

It was summer, a weekday, and midafternoon; no time for any campus Oedipa knew of to be jumping, yet this one was. She came downslope from Wheeler Hall, through Sather Gate into a plaza teeming with corduroy, denim, bare legs, blonde hair, hornrims, bicycle spokes in the sun, bookbags, swaying card tables, long paper petitions dangling to earth, posters for undecipherable FSM's, YAF's, VDC's, suds in the fountain, students in nose-to-nose dialogue. She moved through it carrying her fat book, attracted, unsure, a stranger, wanting to feel relevant but knowing how much of a search among alternate universes it would take. For she had undergone her own educating at a time of nerves, blandness and retreat among not only her fellow students but also most of the visible structure around and ahead of them, this having been a national reflex to certain pathologies in high places only death had had the power to cure, and this Berkeley was like no somnolent Siwash out of her own past at all, but more akin to those Far Eastern or Latin American universities you read about, those autonomous culture media where the most beloved of folklores may be brought into doubt, cataclysmic of dissents voiced, suicidal of commitments chosen—the sort that bring governments down. But it was English she was hearing as she crossed Bancroft Way among the blonde children and the muttering Hondas and Suzukis; American English. Where were Secretaries James and Foster and Senator Joseph, those dear daft numina who'd mothered over Oedipa's so temperate youth? In another world. Along another pattern of track, another string of decisions taken, switches closed, the faceless pointsmen who'd thrown them now all transferred, deserted, in stir, fleeing the skip-tracers, out of their skull, on horse, alcoholic, fanatic, under aliases, dead, impossible to find ever again. Among them they had managed to turn the young Oedipa into a rare creature indeed, unfit perhaps for marches and sit-ins, but just a whiz at pursuing strange words in Jacobean texts.

She pulled the Impala into a gas station somewhere along a gray stretch of Telegraph Avenue and found in a phone book the address of John Nefastis. She then drove to a pseudo-Mexican apartment house, looked for his name among the U. S. mailboxes, ascended outside steps and walked down a row of draped windows till she found his door. He had a crewcut and the same underage look as Koteks, but wore a shirt on various Polynesian themes and dating from the Truman administration.

Introducing herself, she invoked the name of Stanley Koteks. "He said you could tell me whether or not I'm a 'sensitive'."

Nefastis had been watching on his TV set a bunch of kids dancing some kind of a Watusi. "I like to watch young stuff," he explained. "There's something about a little chick that age."

"So does my husband," she said. "I understand."

John Nefastis beamed at her, simpatico, and brought out his Machine from a workroom in back. It looked about the way the patent had described it. "You know how this works?"

"Stanley gave me a kind of rundown."

He began then, bewilderingly, to talk about something called entropy. The word bothered him as much as "Trystero" bothered Oedipa. But it was too technical for her. She did gather that there were two distinct kinds of this entropy. One having to do with heat-engines, the other to do with communication. The equation for one, back in the '30's, had looked very like the equation for the other. It was a coincidence. The two fields were entirely unconnected, except at one point: Maxwell's Demon. As the Demon sat and sorted his molecules into hot and cold, the system was said to lose entropy. But somehow the loss was offset by the information the Demon gained about what molecules were where.

"Communication is the key," cried Nefastis. "The Demon passes his data on to the sensitive, and the sensitive must reply in kind. There are untold billions of molecules in that box. The Demon collects data on each and every one. At some deep psychic level he must get through. The sensitive must receive that staggering set of energies, and feed back something like the same quantity of information. To keep it all cycling. On the secular level all we can see is one piston, hopefully moving. One little movement, against all that massive complex of information, destroyed over and over with each power stroke."

"Help," said Oedipa, "you're not reaching me."

"Entropy is a figure of speech, then," sighed Nefastis, "a metaphor. It connects the world of thermodynamics to the world of information flow. The Machine uses both. The Demon makes the metaphor not only verbally graceful, but also objectively true."

"But what," she felt like some kind of a heretic, "if the Demon exists only because the two equations look alike? Because of the metaphor?"

Nefastis smiled; impenetrable, calm, a believer. "He existed for Clerk Maxwell long before the days of the metaphor."

But had Clerk Maxwell been such a fanatic about his Demon's reality? She looked at the picture on the outside of the box. Clerk Maxwell was in profile and would not meet her eyes. The forehead was round and smooth, and there was a curious bump at the back of his head, covered by curling hair. His visible eye seemed mild and noncommittal, but Oedipa wondered what hangups, crises, spookings in the middle of the night might be developed from the shadowed subtleties of his mouth, hidden under a full beard.

"Watch the picture," said Nefastis, "and concentrate on a cylinder. Don't worry. If you're a sensitive you'll know which one. Leave your mind open, receptive to the Demon's message. I'll be back." He returned to his TV set, which was now showing cartoons. Oedipa sat through two Yogi Bears, one Magilla Gorilla and a Peter Potamus, staring at Clerk Maxwell's enigmatic profile, waiting for the Demon to communicate.

Are you there, little fellow, Oedipa asked the Demon, or is Nefastis putting me on. Unless a piston moved, she'd never know. Clerk Maxwell's hands were cropped out of the photo-graph. He might have been holding a book. He gazed away, into some vista of Victorian England whose light had been lost for-ever. Oedipa's anxiety grew. It seemed, behind the beard, he'd begun, ever so faintly, to smile. Something in his eyes, certainly, had changed . . .

And there. At the top edge of what she could see: hadn't the right-hand piston moved, a fraction? She couldn't look directly, the instructions were to keep her eyes on Clerk Maxwell. Minutes passed, pistons remained frozen in place. High-pitched, comic voices issued from the TV set. She had seen only a retinal twitch, a misfired nerve cell. Did the true sensitive see more? In her colon now she was afraid, growing more so, that nothing would hap-pen. Why worry, she worried; Nefastis is a nut, forget it, a sincere nut. The true sensitive is the one that can share in the man's hallu-cinations, that's all.

How wonderful they might be to share. For fifteen minutes more she tried; repeating, if you are there, whatever you are, show yourself to me, I need you, show yourself. But nothing happened.

"I'm sorry," she called in, surprisingly about to cry with frus-tration, her voice breaking. "It's no use." Nefastis came to her and put an arm around her shoulders.

"It's OK," he said. "Please don't cry. Come on in on the couch. The news will be on any minute. We can do it there."

"It?" said Oedipa. "Do it? What?"

"Have sexual intercourse," replied Nefastis. "Maybe there'll be something about China tonight. I like to do it while they talk about Viet Nam, but China is best of all. You think about all those Chinese. Teeming. That profusion of life. It makes it sexier, right?"

"Gah," Oedipa screamed, and fled, Nefastis snapping his

fingers through the dark rooms behind her in a hippy-dippy, oh-go-ahead-then-chick fashion he had doubtless learned from watching the TV also.

"Say hello to old Stanley," he called as she pattered down the steps into the street, flung a babushka over her license plate and screeched away down Telegraph. She drove more or less automatically until a swift boy in a Mustang, perhaps unable to contain the new sense of virility his auto gave him, nearly killed her and she realized that she was on the freeway, heading irreversibly for the Bay Bridge. It was the middle of rush hour. Oedipa was appalled at the spectacle, having thought such traffic only possible in Los Angeles, places like that. Looking down at San Francisco a few minutes later from the high point of the bridge's arc, she saw smog. Haze, she corrected herself, is what it is, haze. How can they have smog in San Francisco? Smog, according to the folklore, did not begin till farther south. It had to be the angle of the sun.

Amid the exhaust, sweat, glare and ill-humor of a summer evening on an American freeway, Oedipa Maas pondered her Trystero problem. All the silence of San Narciso—the calm surface of the motel pool, the contemplative contours of residential streets like rakings in the sand of a Japanese garden—had not allowed her to think as leisurely as this freeway madness.

For John Nefastis (to take a recent example) two kinds of entropy, thermodynamic and informational, happened, say by coincidence, to look alike, when you wrote them down as equations. Yet he had made his mere coincidence respectable, with the help of Maxwell's Demon.

Now here was Oedipa, faced with a metaphor of God knew how many parts; more than two, anyway. With coincidences blossoming these days wherever she looked, she had nothing but a sound, a word, Trystero, to hold them together.

She knew a few things about it: it had opposed the Thurn and Taxis postal system in Europe; its symbol was a muted post horn; sometime before 1853 it had appeared in America and fought the Pony Express and Wells, Fargo, either as outlaws in black, or disguised as Indians; and it survived today, in California, serving as a channel of communication for those of unorthodox sexual persuasion, inventors who believed in the reality of Maxwell's Demon, possibly her own husband, Mucho Maas (but she'd thrown Mucho's letter long away, there was no way for Genghis Cohen to check the stamp, so if she wanted to find out for sure she'd have to ask Mucho himself).

Either Trystero did exist, in its own right, or it was being presumed, perhaps fantasied by Oedipa, so hung up on and interpenetrated with the dead man's estate. Here in San Francisco, away from all tangible assets of that estate, there might still be a chance of getting the whole thing to go away and disintegrate quietly. She had only to drift tonight, at random, and watch nothing happen, to be convinced it was purely nervous, a little something for her shrink to fix. She got off the freeway at North Beach, drove around, parked finally in a steep side-street among warehouses. Then walked along Broadway, into the first crowds of evening.

But it took her no more than an hour to catch sight of a muted post horn. She was moseying along a street full of aging boys in Roos Atkins suits when she collided with a gang of guided tourists come rowdy-dowing out of a Volkswagen bus, on route to take in a few San Francisco nite spots. "Let me lay this on you," a voice spoke into her ear, "because I just left," and she found being deftly pinned outboard of one breast this big cerise ID badge, reading HI! MY NAME IS **Arnold Snarb!** AND I'M LOOKIN' FOR A GOOD TIME! Oedipa glanced around and saw a cherubic face vanishing with a wink in among natural shoulders and striped shirts, and away went Arnold Snarb, looking for a better time.

Somebody blew on an athletic whistle and Oedipa found herself being herded, along with other badged citizens, toward a bar called The Greek Way. Oh, no, Oedipa thought, not a fag joint, no; and for a minute tried to fight out of the human surge, before recalling how she had decided to drift tonight.

"Now in here," their guide, sweating dark tentacles into his tab collar, briefed them, "you are going to see the members of the third sex, the lavender crowd this city by the Bay is so justly famous for. To some of you the experience may seem a little queer, but remember, try not to act like a bunch of tourists. If you get propositioned it'll all be in fun, just part of the gay night life to be found here in famous North Beach. Two drinks and when you hear the whistle it means out, on the double, regroup right here. If you're well behaved we'll hit Finocchio's next." He blew the whistle twice and the tourists, breaking into a yell, swept Oedipa inside, in a frenzied assault on the bar. When things had calmed she was near the door with an unidentifiable drink in her fist, jammed against somebody tall in a suede sport coat. In the lapel of which she spied, wrought exquisitely in some pale, glimmering alloy, not another cerise badge, but a pin in the shape of the Trystero post horn. Mute and everything.

All right, she told herself. You lose. A game try, all one hour's worth. She should have left then and gone back to Berkeley, to the hotel. But couldn't.

"What if I told you," she addressed the owner of the pin, "that I was an agent of Thurn and Taxis?"

"What," he answered, "some theatrical agency?" He had large ears, hair cropped nearly to his scalp, acne on his face, and curiously empty eyes, which now swiveled briefly to Oedipa's breasts. "How'd you get a name like Arnold Snarb?"

"If you tell me where you got your lapel pin," said Oedipa.

"Sorry."

She sought to bug him: "If it's a homosexual sign or something, that doesn't bother me."

Eyes showing nothing: "I don't swing that way," he said. "Yours either." Turned his back on her and ordered a drink. Oedipa took off her badge, put it in an ashtray and said, quietly, trying not to suggest hysteria,

"Look, you have to help me. Because I really think I am going out of my head."

"You have the wrong outfit, Arnold. Talk to your clergyman."

"I use the U. S. Mail because I was never taught any different," she pleaded. "But I'm not your enemy. I don't want to be."

"What about my friend?" He came spinning around on the stool to face her again. "You want to be that, Arnold?"

"I don't know," she thought she'd better say.

He looked at her, blank. "What *do* you know?"

She told him everything. Why not? Held nothing back. At the end of it the tourists had been whistled away and he'd bought two rounds to Oedipa's three.

"I'd heard about 'Kirby,'" he said, "it's a code name, nobody real. But none of the rest, your Sinophile across the bay, or that sick play. I never thought there was a history to it."

"I think of nothing but," she said, and a little plaintive.

"And," scratching the stubble on his head, "you have nobody else to tell this to. Only somebody in a bar whose name you don't know?"

She wouldn't look at him. "I guess not."

"No husband, no shrink?"

"Both," Oedipa said, "but they don't know."

"You can't tell them?"

She met his eyes' void for a second after all, and shrugged.

"I'll tell you what I know, then," he decided. "The pin I'm wearing means I'm a member of the IA. That's Inamorati Anonymous. An inamorato is somebody in love. That's the worst addiction of all."

"Somebody is about to fall in love," Oedipa said, "you go sit with them, or something?"

"Right. The whole idea is to get to where you don't need it. I was lucky. I kicked it young. But there are sixty-year-old men, believe it or not, and women even older, who wake up in the night screaming."

"You hold meetings, then, like the AA?"

"No, of course not. You get a phone number, an answering service you can call. Nobody knows anybody else's name; just the number in case it gets so bad you can't handle it alone. We're isolates, Arnold. Meetings would destroy the whole point of it."

"What about the person who comes to sit with you? Suppose you fall in love with them?"

"They go away," he said. "You never see them twice. The answering service dispatches them, and they're careful not to have any repeats."

How did the post horn come in? That went back to their founding. In the early '60's a Yoyodyne executive living near L.A. and located someplace in the corporate root-system above supervisor but below vice-president, found himself, at age 39, automated out of a job. Having been since age 7 rigidly instructed in an eschatology that pointed nowhere but to a presidency and death, trained to do absolutely nothing but sign his name to specialized memoranda he could not begin to understand and to take blame for the running-amok of specialized programs that failed for specialized reasons he had to have explained to him, the executive's first thoughts were naturally of suicide. But previous training got the better of him: he could not make the decision without first hearing the ideas of a committee. He placed an ad in the personal column of the L.A. *Times,* asking whether anyone who'd been in the same fix had ever found any good reasons for not committing suicide. His shrewd assumption being that no suicides would reply, leaving him automatically with only valid inputs. The assumption was false. After a week of anxiously watching the mailbox through little Japanese binoculars his wife had given him for a going away present (she'd left him the day after he was pink-slipped) and getting nothing but sucker-list stuff through the regular deliveries that came each noon, he was jolted out of a boozy, black-and-white dream of jumping off The Stack into rush-hour traffic, by an insistent banging at the door. It was late on a Sunday afternoon. He opened his door and found an aged bum with a knitted watch cap on his head and a hook for a hand, who presented him with a bundle of letters and loped away without a word. Most of the letters were from suicides who had failed, either through clumsiness or last-minute cowardice. None of them, however, could offer any compelling reasons for staying alive. Still the executive dithered: spent another week with pieces of paper on which he would list, in columns headed "pro" and "con," reasons for and against taking his Brody. He found it impossible, in the absence of some trigger, to come to any clear decision. Finally one day he noticed a front page story in the *Times,* complete with AP wirephoto, about a Buddhist monk in Viet Nam who had set himself on fire to protest government policies. "Groovy!" cried the executive. He went to the garage, siphoned all the gasoline from his Buick's tank, put on his green Zachary All suit with the vest, stuffed all his letters from unsuccessful suicides into a coat pocket, went in the kitchen, sat on the floor, proceeded to douse himself good with the gasoline. He was about to make the farewell flick of the wheel on his faithful

Zippo, which had seen him through the Normany hedgerows, the Ardennes, Germany, and postwar America, when he heard a key in the front door, and voices. It was his wife and some man, whom he soon recognized as the very efficiency expert at Yoyodyne who had caused him to be replaced by an IBM 7094. Intrigued by the irony of it, he sat in the kitchen and listened, leaving his necktie dipped in the gasoline as a sort of wick. From what he could gather, the efficiency expert wished to have sexual intercourse with the wife on the Moroccan rug in the living room. The wife was not unwilling. The executive heard lewd laughter, zippers, the thump of shoes, heavy breathing, moans. He took his tie out of the gasoline and started to snigger. He closed the top on his Zippo. "I hear laughing," his wife said presently. "I smell gasoline," said the efficiency expert. Hand in hand, naked, the two proceeded to the kitchen. "I was about to do the Buddhist monk thing," explained the executive. "Nearly three weeks it takes him," marvelled the efficiency expert, "to decide. You know how long it would've taken the IBM 7094? Twelve microseconds. No wonder you were replaced." The executive threw back his head and laughed for a solid ten minutes, along toward the middle of which his wife and her friend, alarmed, retired, got dressed and went out looking for the police. The executive undressed, showered and hung his suit out on the line to dry. Then he noticed a curious thing. The stamps on some of the letters in his suit pocket had turned almost white. He realized that the gasoline must have dissolved the printing ink. Idly, he peeled off a stamp and saw suddenly the image of the muted post horn, the skin of his hand showing clearly through the watermark. "A sign," he whispered, "is what it is." If he'd been a religious man he would have fallen to his knees. As it was, he only declared, with great solemnity: "My big mistake was love. From this day I swear to stay off of love: hetero, homo, bi, dog or cat, car, every kind there is. I will found a society of isolates, dedicated to this purpose, and this sign, revealed by the same gasoline that almost destroyed me, will be its emblem." And he did.

Oedipa, by now rather drunk, said, "Where is he now?"

"He's anonymous," said the anonymous inamorato. "Why not write to him through your WASTE system? Say 'Founder, IA.'"

"But I don't know how to use it," she said.

"Think of it," he went on, also drunk. "A whole underworld of suicides who failed. All keeping in touch through that secret delivery system. What do they tell each other?" He shook his head, smiling, stumbled off his stool and headed off to take a leak, disappearing into the dense crowd. He didn't come back.

Oedipa sat, feeling as alone as she ever had, now the only woman, she saw, in a room full of drunken male homosexuals. Story of my life, she thought, Mucho won't talk to me, Hilarius won't listen, Clerk Maxwell didn't even look at me, and this group, God knows. Despair came over her, as it will when nobody around has any sexual relevance to you. She gauged the spectrum of feeling out there as running from really violent hate (an Indian-looking kid hardly out of his teens, with frosted shoulder-length hair tucked behind his ears and pointed cowboy boots) to dry speculation (a hornrimmed SS type who stared at her legs, trying to figure out if she was in drag), none of which could do her any good. So she got up after awhile and left The Greek Way, and entered the city again, the infected city.

And spent the rest of the night finding the image of the Trystero post horn. In Chinatown, in the dark window of a herbalist, she thought she saw it on a sign among ideographs. But the streetlight was dim. Later, on a sidewalk, she saw two of them in chalk, 20 feet apart. Between them a complicated array of boxes, some with letters, some with numbers. A kids' game? Places on a map, dates from a secret history? She copied the diagram in her memo book. When she looked up, a man, perhaps a man, in a black suit, was standing in a doorway half a block away, watching her. She thought she saw a turned-around collar but took no chances; headed back the way she'd come, pulse thundering. A bus stopped at the next corner, and she ran to catch it.

She stayed with buses after that, getting off only now and then to walk so she'd keep awake. What fragments of dreams came had to do with the post horn. Later, possibly, she would have trouble sorting the night into real and dreamed.

At some indefinite passage in night's sonorous score, it also came to her that she would be safe, that something, perhaps only her linearly fading drunkenness, would protect her. The city was hers, as, made up and sleeked so with the customary words and images (cosmopolitan, culture, cable cars) it had not been before: she had safe-passage tonight to its far blood's branchings, be they capillaries too small for more than peering into, or vessels mashed together in shameless municipal hickeys, out on the skin for all but tourists to see. Nothing of the night's could touch her; nothing did. The repetition of symbols was to be enough, without trauma as well perhaps to attenuate it or even jar it altogether loose from her memory. *She was meant to remember.* She faced that possibility as she might the toy street from a high balcony, roller-coaster ride, feeding-time among the beasts in a zoo—any death-wish that can be consummated by some minimum gesture. She touched the edge of its voluptuous field, knowing it would be lovely beyond dreams simply to submit to it; that not gravity's pull, laws of ballistics, feral ravening, promised more delight. She tested it, shivering: I am meant to remember. Each clue that comes is *supposed* to have its own clarity, its fine chances for per- manence. But then she wondered if the gemlike "clues" were only some kind of compensation. To make up for her having lost the direct, epileptic Word, the cry that might abolish the night.

In Golden Gate Park she came on a circle of children in their nightclothes, who told her they were dreaming the gathering. But that the dream was really no different from being awake, because in the mornings when they got up they felt tired, as if they'd been up most of the night. When their mothers thought they were out playing they were really curled in cupboards of neighbors' houses, in platforms up in trees, in secretly-hollowed nests inside hedges, sleeping, making up for these hours. The night was empty of all terror for them, they had inside their circle an imaginary fire, and needed nothing but their own unpenetrated sense of community. They knew about the post horn, but nothing of the chalked game Oedipa had seen on the sidewalk. You used only one image and it was a jump-rope game, a little girl explained: you stepped alternately in the loop, the bell, and the mute, while your girlfriend sang:

> *Tristoe, Tristoe, one, two, three,*
> *Turning taxi from across the sea . . .*

"Thurn and Taxis, you mean?"

They'd never heard it that way. Went on warming their hands at an invisible fire. Oedipa, to retaliate, stopped believing in them.

In an all-night Mexican greasy spoon off 24th, she found a piece of her past, in the form of one Jesús Arrabal, who was sitting in a corner under the TV set, idly stirring his bowl of opaque soup with the foot of a chicken. "Hey," he greeted Oedipa, "you were the lady in Mazatlán." He beckoned her to sit.

"You remember everything," Oedipa said, "Jesús; even tourists. How is your CIA?" Standing not for the agency you think, but for a clandestine Mexican outfit known as the Conjuración de los Insurgentes Anarquistas, traceable back to the time of the Flores Magón brothers and later briefly allied with Zapata.

"You see. In exile," waving his arm around at the place. He was part-owner here with a yucateco who still believed in the Revolution. *Their* Revolution. "And you. Are you still with that gringo who spent too much money on you? The oligarchist, the miracle?"

"He died."

"Ah, pobrecito." They had met Jesús Arrabal on the beach, where he had previously announced an antigovernment rally. Nobody had showed up. So he fell to talking to Inverarity, the enemy he must, to be true to his faith, learn. Pierce, because of his neutral manners when in the presence of ill-will, had nothing to tell Arrabal; he played the rich, obnoxious gringo so perfectly that Oedipa had seen gooseflesh come up along the anarchist's forearms, due to no Pacific sea-breeze. Soon as Pierce went off to sport in the surf, Arrabal asked her if he was real, or a spy, or making fun of him. Oedipa didn't understand.

"You know what a miracle is. Not what Bakunin said. But another world's intrusion into this one. Most of the time we coexist peacefully, but when we do touch there's cataclysm. Like the church we hate, anarchists also believe in another world. Where revolutions break out spontaneous and leaderless, and the soul's talent for consensus allows the masses to work together without effort, automatic as the body itself. And yet, señá, if any of it should ever really happen that perfectly, I would also have to cry miracle. An anarchist miracle. Like your friend. He is too exactly and without flaw the thing we fight. In Mexico the privilegiado is always, to a finite percentage, redeemed—one of the people. Unmiraculous. But your friend, unless he's joking, is as terrifying to me as a Virgin appearing to an Indian."

In the years intervening Oedipa had remembered Jesús because he'd seen that about Pierce and she hadn't. As if he were, in some unsexual way, competition. Now, drinking thick lukewarm coffee from a clay pot on the back burner of the yucateco's stove and listening to Jesús talk conspiracy, she wondered if, without the miracle of Pierce to reassure him, Jesús might not have quit his CIA eventually and gone over like everybody else to the majority priistas, and so never had to go into exile.

The dead man, like Maxwell's Demon, was the linking feature in a coincidence. Without him neither she nor Jesús would be exactly here, exactly now. It was enough, a coded warning. What, tonight, was chance? So her eyes did fall presently onto an ancient rolled copy of the anarcho-syndicalist paper *Regeneración*. The date was 1904 and there was no stamp next to the cancellation, only the handstruck image of the post horn.

"They arrive," said Arrabal. "Have they been in the mails that long? Has my name been substituted for that of a member who's died? Has it really taken sixty years? Is it a reprint? Idle questions, I am a footsoldier. The higher levels have their reasons." She carried this thought back out into the night with her.

Down at the city beach, long after the pizza stands and rides had closed, she walked unmolested through a drifting, dreamy cloud of delinquents in summer-weight gang jackets with the post horn stitched on in thread that looked pure silver in what moonlight there was. They had all been smoking, snuffing or injecting something, and perhaps did not see her at all.

Riding among an exhausted busful of Negroes going on to graveyard shifts all over the city, she saw scratched on the back of a seat, shining for her in the brilliant smoky interior, the post horn with the legend DEATH. But unlike WASTE, somebody had troubled to write in, in pencil: DON'T EVER ANTAGONIZE THE HORN.

Somewhere near Fillmore she found the symbol tacked to the bulletin board of a laundromat, among other scraps of paper offering cheap ironing and baby sitters. *If you know what this means,* the note said, *you know where to find out more.* Around her the odor of chlorine bleach rose heavenward, like an incense. Machines chugged and sloshed fiercely. Except for Oedipa the place was deserted, and the fluorescent bulbs seemed to shriek whiteness, to which everything their light touched was dedicated. It was a Negro neighborhood. Was The Horn so dedicated? Would it Antagonize The Horn to ask? Who could she ask?

In the buses all night she listened to transistor radios playing songs in the lower stretches of the Top 200, that would never become popular, whose melodies and lyrics would perish as if they had never been sung. A Mexican girl, trying to hear one of these through snarling static from the bus's motor, hummed along as if she would remember it always, tracing post horns and hearts with a fingernail, in the haze of her breath on the window.

Out at the airport Oedipa, feeling invisible, eavesdropped on a poker game whose steady loser entered each loss neat and conscientious in a little balance-book decorated inside with scrawled post horns. "I'm averaging a 99.375 percent return, fellas," she heard him say. The others, strangers, looked at him, some blank, some annoyed. "That's averaging it out, over 23 years," he went on, trying a smile. "Always just that little percent on the wrong side of breaking even. Twenty-three years. I'll never get ahead of it. Why don't I quit?" Nobody answering.

In one of the latrines was an advertisement by ACDC, standing for Alameda County Death Cult, along with a box number and post horn. Once a month they were to choose some victim from among the innocent, the virtuous, the socially integrated and well-adjusted, using him sexually, then sacrificing him. Oedipa did not copy the number.

Catching a TWA flight to Miami was an uncoordinated boy who planned to slip at night into aquariums and open negotiations with the dolphins, who would succeed man. He was kissing his mother passionately goodbye, using his tongue. "I'll write, ma," he kept saying. "Write by WASTE," she said, "remember. The government will open it if you use the other. The dolphins will be mad." "I love you, ma," he said. "Love the dolphins," she advised him. "Write by WASTE."

So it went. Oedipa played the voyeur and listener. Among her other encounters were a facially-deformed welder, who cherished his ugliness; a child roaming the night who missed the death before birth as certain outcasts do the dear lulling blankness of the community; a Negro woman with an intricately-marbled scar along the baby-fat of one cheek who kept going through rituals of miscarriage each for a different reason, deliberately as others might the ritual of birth, dedicated not to continuity but to some kind of interregnum; an aging night-watchman, nibbling at a bar of Ivory Soap, who had trained his virtuoso stomach to accept also lotions, air-fresheners, fabrics, tobaccoes and waxes in a hopeless attempt to assimilate it all, all the promise, productivity, betrayal, ulcers, before it was too late; and even another voyeur, who hung outside one of the city's still-lighted windows, searching for who knew what specific image. Decorating each alienation, each species of withdrawal, as cufflink, decal, aimless doodling, there was somehow always the post horn. She grew so to expect it that perhaps she did not see it quite as often as she later was to remember seeing it. A couple-three times would really have been enough. Or too much.

She busrode and walked on into the lightening morning, giving herself up to a fatalism rare for her. Where was the Oedipa who'd driven so bravely up here from San Narciso? That optimistic baby had come on so like the private eye in any long-ago radio drama, believing all you needed was grit, resourcefulness, exemption from hidebound cops' rules, to solve any great mystery.

But the private eye sooner or later has to get beat up on.

This night's profusion of post horns, this malignant, deliberate replication, was their way of beating up. They knew her pressure points, and the ganglia of her optimism, and one by one, pinch by precision pinch, they were immobilizing her.

Last night, she might have wondered what undergrounds apart from the couple she knew of communicated by WASTE system. By sunrise she could legitimately ask what undergrounds didn't. If miracles were, as Jesús Arrabal had postulated years ago on the beach at Mazatlán, intrusions into this world from another, a kiss of cosmic pool balls, then so must be each of the night's post horns. For here were God knew how many citizens, deliberately choosing not to communicate by U. S. Mail. It was not an act of treason, nor possibly even of defiance. But it was a calculated withdrawal, from the life of the Republic, from its machinery. Whatever else was being denied them out of hate, indifference to the power of their vote, loopholes, simple ignorance, this withdrawal was their own, unpublicized, private. Since they could not have withdrawn into a vacuum (could they?), there had to exist the separate, silent, unsuspected world.

Just before the morning rush hour, she got out of a jitney whose ancient driver ended each day in the red, downtown on Howard Street, began to walk toward the Embarcadero. She knew she looked terrible—knuckles black with eye-liner and mascara from where she'd rubbed, mouth tasting of old booze and coffee. Through an open doorway, on the stair leading up into the disinfectant-smelling twilight of a rooming house she saw an old man huddled, shaking with grief she couldn't hear. Both hands, smoke-white, covered his face. On the back of the left hand she made out the post horn, tattooed in old ink now beginning to blur and spread. Fascinated, she came into the shadows and ascended creaking steps, hesitating on each one. When she was three steps from him the hands flew apart and his wrecked face, and the terror of eyes gloried in burst veins, stopped her.

"Can I help?" She was shaking, tired.

"My wife's in Fresno," he said. He wore an old double-breasted suit, frayed gray shirt, wide tie, no hat. "I left her. So long ago, I don't remember. Now this is for her." He gave Oedipa a letter that looked like he'd been carrying it around for years. "Drop it in the," and he held up the tattoo and stared into her eyes, "you know. I can't go out there. It's too far now, I had a bad night."

"I know," she said. "But I'm new in town. I don't know where it is."

"Under the freeway." He waved her on in the direction she'd been going. "Always one. You'll see it." The eyes closed. Cammed each night out of that safe furrow the bulk of this city's waking each sunrise again set virtuously to plowing, what rich soils had he turned, what concentric planets uncovered? What voices overheard, flinders of luminescent gods glimpsed among the wallpaper's stained foliage, candlestubs lit to rotate in the air over him, prefiguring the cigarette he or a friend must fall asleep someday smoking, thus to end among the flaming, secret salts held all those years by the insatiable stuffing of a mattress that could keep vestiges of every nightmare sweat, helpless overflowing bladder, viciously, tearfully consummated wet dream, like the memory bank to a computer of the lost? She was overcome all at once by a need to touch him, as if she could not believe in him, or would not remember him, without it. Exhausted, hardly knowing what she was doing, she came the last three steps and sat, took the man in her arms, actually held him, gazing out of her smudged eyes down the stairs, back into the morning. She felt wetness against her breast and saw that he was crying again. He hardly breathed but tears came as if being pumped. "I can't help," she whispered, rocking him, "I can't help." It was already too many miles to Fresno.

"Is that him?" a voice asked behind her, up the stairs. "The sailor?"

"He has a tattoo on his hand."

"Can you bring him up OK? That's him." She turned and saw an even older man, shorter, wearing a tall Homburg hat and smiling at them. "I'd help you but I got a little arthritis."

"Does he have to come up?" she said. "Up there?"

"Where else, lady?"

She didn't know. She let go of him for a moment, reluctant as if he were her own child, and he looked up at her. "Come on," she said. He reached out the tattooed hand and she took that, and that was how they went the rest of the way up that flight, and then the two more: hand in hand, very slowly for the man with arthritis.

"He disappeared last night," he told her. "Said he was going looking for his old lady. It's a thing he does, off and on." They entered a warren of rooms and corridors, lit by 10-watt bulbs, separated by beaverboard partitions. The old man followed them stiffly. At last he said, "Here."

In the little room were another suit, a couple of religious tracts, a rug, a chair. A picture of a saint, changing well-water to oil for Jerusalem's Easter lamps. Another bulb, dead. The bed. The mattress, waiting. She ran through then a scene she might play. She might find the landlord of this place, and bring him to court, and buy the sailor a new suit at Roos/Atkins, and shirt, and shoes, and give him the bus fare to Fresno after all. But with a sigh he had released her hand, while she was so lost in the fantasy that she hadn't felt it go away, as if he'd known the best moment to let go.

"Just mail the letter," he said, "the stamp is on it." She looked and saw the familiar carmine 8¢ airmail, with a jet flying by the Capitol dome. But at the top of the dome stood a tiny figure in deep black, with its arms outstretched. Oedipa wasn't sure what exactly was supposed to be on top of the Capitol, but knew it wasn't anything like that.

"Please," the sailor said. "Go on now. You don't want to stay here." She looked in her purse, found a ten and a single, gave him the ten. "I'll spend it on booze," he said.

"Remember your friends," said the arthritic, watching the ten.

"Bitch," said the sailor. "Why didn't you wait till he was gone?"

Oedipa watched him make adjustments so he'd fit easier against the mattress. That stuffed memory. Register A . . .

"Give me a cigarette, Ramírez," the sailor said. "I know you got one."

Would it be today? "Ramírez," she cried. The arthritic looked around on his rusty neck. "He's going to die," she said.

"Who isn't?" said Ramírez.

She remembered John Nefastis, talking about his Machine, and massive destructions of information. So when this mattress flared up around the sailor, in his Viking's funeral: the stored, coded years of uselessness, early death, self-harrowing, the sure decay of hope, the set of all men who had slept on it, whatever their lives had been, would truly cease to be, forever, when the mattress burned. She stared at it in wonder. It was as if she had just discovered the irreversible process. It astonished her to think that so much could be lost, even the quantity of hallucination belonging just to the sailor that the world would bear no further trace of. She knew, because she had held him, that he suffered DT's. Behind the initials was a metaphor, a delirium tremens, a trembling unfurrowing of the mind's plowshare. The saint whose water can light lamps, the clairvoyant whose lapse in recall is the breath of God, the true paranoid for whom all is organized in spheres joyful or threatening about the central pulse of himself, the dreamer whose puns probe ancient fetid shafts and tunnels of truth all act in the same special relevance to the word, or whatever it is the word is there, buffering, to protect us from. The act of metaphor then was a thrust at truth and a lie, depending where you were: inside, safe, or outside, lost. Oedipa did not know where she was. Trembling, unfurrowed, she slipped sidewise, screeching back across grooves of years, to hear again the earnest, high voice of her second or third collegiate love Ray Glozing bitching among "uhs" and the syncopated tonguing of a cavity, about his freshman calculus; "dt," God help this old tattooed man, meant also a time differential, a vanishingly small instant in which change had to be confronted at last for what it was, where it could no longer disguise itself as something innocuous like an average rate; where velocity dwelled in the projectile though the projectile be frozen in midflight, where death dwelled in the cell though the cell be looked in on at its most quick. She knew that the sailor had seen worlds no other man had seen if only because there was that high magic to low puns, because DT's must give access to dt's of spectra beyond the known sun, music made purely of Antarctic loneliness and fright. But nothing she knew of would preserve them, or him. She gave him goodbye, walked downstairs and then on, in the direction he'd told her. For an hour she prowled among the sunless, concrete underpinnings of the freeway, finding drunks, bums, pedestrians, pederasts, hookers, walking psychotic, no secret mailbox. But at last in the shadows she did come on a can with a swinging trapezoidal top, the kind you throw trash in: old and green, nearly four feet high. On the swinging part were hand-painted the initials W.A.S.T.E. She had to look closely to see the periods between the letters.

Oedipa settled back in the shadow of a column. She may have dozed off. She woke to see a kid dropping a bundle of letters into the can. She went over and dropped in the sailor's letter to Fresno; then hid again and waited. Toward midday a rangy young wino showed up with a sack; unlocked a panel at the side of the box and took out all the letters. Oedipa gave him half a block's start, then began to tail him. Congratulating herself on having thought to wear flats, at least. The carrier led her across Market then over toward City Hall. In a street close enough to the drab, stone openness of the Civic Center to be infected by its gray, he rendezvoused with another carrier, and they exchanged sacks. Oedipa decided to stick with the one she'd been following. She tailed him all the way back down the littered, shifty, loud length of Market and over on First Street to the trans-bay bus terminal, where he bought a ticket for Oakland. So did Oedipa.

They rode over the bridge and into the great, empty glare of the Oakland afternoon. The landscape lost all variety. The carrier got off in a neighborhood Oedipa couldn't identify. She followed him for hours along streets whose names she never knew, across arterials that even with the afternoon's lull nearly murdered her, into slums and out, up long hillsides jammed solid with two- or three-bedroom houses, all their windows giving blankly back only the sun. One by one his sack of letters emptied. At length he climbed on a Berkeley bus. Oedipa followed. Halfway up Telegraph the carrier got off and led her down the street to a pseudo-Mexican apartment house. Not once had he looked behind him. John Nefastis lived here. She was back where she'd started, and could not believe 24 hours had passed. Should it have been more or less?

Back in the hotel she found the lobby full of deaf-mute delegates in party hats, copied in crepe paper after the fur Chinese communist jobs made popular during the Korean conflict. They were every one of them drunk, and a few of the men grabbed her, thinking to bring her along to a party in the grand ballroom. She tried to struggle out of the silent, gesturing swarm, but was too weak. Her legs ached, her mouth tasted horrible. They swept her on into the ballroom, where she was seized about the waist by a handsome young man in a Harris tweed coat and waltzed round and round, through the rustling, shuffling hush, under a great unlit chandelier. Each couple on the floor danced whatever was in the fellow's head: tango, two-step, bossa nova, slop. But how long, Oedipa thought, could it go on before collisions became a serious hindrance? There would have to be collisions. The only alternative was some unthinkable order of music, many rhythms, all keys at once, a choreography in which each couple meshed easy, predestined. Something they all heard with an extra sense atrophied in herself. She followed her partner's lead, limp in the young mute's clasp, waiting for the collisions to begin. But none came. She was danced for half an hour before, by mysterious consensus, everybody took a break, without having felt any touch but the touch of her partner. Jesús Arrabal would have called it an anarchist miracle. Oedipa, with no name for it, was only demoralized. She curtsied and fled.

Next day, after twelve hours of sleep and no dreams to speak of, Oedipa checked out of the hotel and drove down the peninsula to Kinneret. She had decided on route, with time to think about the day preceding, to go see Dr Hilarius her shrink, and tell him all. She might well be in the cold and sweatless meathooks of a psychosis. With her own eyes she had verified a WASTE system: seen two WASTE postmen, a WASTE mailbox, WASTE stamps, WASTE cancellations. And the image of the muted post horn all but saturating the Bay Area. Yet she wanted it all to be fantasy—some clear result of her several wounds, needs, dark doubles. She wanted Hilarius to tell her she was some kind of a nut and needed a rest, and that there was no Trystero. She also wanted to know why the chance of its being real should menace her so.

She pulled into the drive at Hilarius's clinic a little after sunset. The light in his office didn't seem to be on. Eucalyptus branches blew in a great stream of air that flowed downhill, sucked to the evening sea. Halfway along the flagstone path, she was startled by an insect whirring loudly past her ear, followed at once by the sound of a gunshot. That was no insect, thought Oedipa, at which point, hearing another shot, she made the connection. In the fading light she was a clear target; the only way to go was toward the clinic. She dashed up to the glass doors, found them locked, the lobby inside dark. Oedipa picked up a rock next to a flower bed and heaved it at one of the doors. It bounced off. She was looking around for another rock when a white shape appeared inside, fluttering up to the door and unlocking it for her. It was Helga Blamm, Hilarius's sometime assistant.

"Hurry," she chattered, as Oedipa slipped inside. The woman was close to hysterical.

"What's happening?" Oedipa said.

"He's gone crazy. I tried to call the police, but he took a chair and smashed the switchboard with it."

"Dr Hilarius?"

"He thinks someone's after him." Tear streaks had meandered down over the nurse's cheekbones. "He's locked himself in the office with that rifle." A Gewehr 43, from the war, Oedipa recalled, that he kept as a souvenir.

"He shot at me. Do you think anybody will report it?"

"Well he's shot at half a dozen people," replied Nurse Blamm, leading Oedipa down a corridor to her office. "Somebody better report it." Oedipa noticed that the window opened on a safe line of retreat.

"You could've run," she said.

Blamm, running hot water from a washbasin tap into cups and stirring in instant coffee, looked up, quizzical. "He might need somebody."

"Who's supposed to be after him?"

"Three men with submachine guns, he said. Terrorists, fanatics, that was all I got. He started breaking up the PBX." She gave Oedipa a hostile look. "Too many nutty broads, that's what did it. Kinneret is full of nothing but. He couldn't cope."

"I've been away for a while," Oedipa said. "Maybe I could find out what it is. Maybe I'd be less of a threat for him."

Blamm burned her mouth on the coffee. "Start telling him your troubles and he'll probably shoot you."

In front of his door, which she could never remember having seen closed, Oedipa stood hipshot awhile, questioning her own sanity. Why hadn't she split out through Blamm's window and read about the rest of it in the paper?

"Who is it?" Hilarius screamed, having picked up her breathing, or something.

"Mrs. Maas."

"May Speer and his ministry of cretins rot eternally in hell. Do you realize that half these rounds are duds?"

"May I come in? Could we talk?"

"I'm sure you'd all like that," Hilarius said.

"I'm unarmed. You can frisk me."

"While you karate-chop me in the spine, no thank you."

"Why are you resisting every suggestion I make?"

"Listen," Hilarius said after awhile, "have I seemed to you a good enough Freudian? Have I ever deviated seriously?"

"You made faces now and then," said Oedipa, "but that's minor."

His response was a long, bitter laugh. Oedipa waited. "I tried," the shrink behind the door said, "to submit myself to that man, to the ghost of that cantankerous Jew. Tried to cultivate a faith in the literal truth of everything he wrote, even the idiocies and contradictions. It was the least I could have done, nicht wahr? A kind of penance.

"And part of me must have really wanted to believe—like a child hearing, in perfect safety, a tale of horror—that the unconscious would be like any other room, once the light was let in. That the dark shapes would resolve only into toy horses and Biedermeyer furniture. That therapy could tame it after all, bring it into society with no fear of its someday reverting. I wanted to believe, despite everything my life had been. Can you imagine?"

She could not, having no idea what Hilarius had done before showing up in Kinneret. Far away she now heard sirens, the electronic kind the local cops used, that sounded like a slide-whistle being played over a P.A. system. With linear obstinacy they grew louder.

"Yes, I hear them," Hilarius said. "Do you think anyone can protect me from these fanatics? They walk through walls. They replicate: you flee them, turn a corner, and there they are, coming for you again."

"Do me a favor?" Oedipa said. "Don't shoot at the cops, they're on your side."

"Your Israeli has access to every uniform known," Hilarius said. "I can't guarantee the safety of the 'police.' You couldn't guarantee where they'd take me if I surrendered, could you."

She heard him pacing around his office. Unearthly siren-sounds converged on them from all over the night. "There is a face," Hilarius said, "that I can make. One you haven't seen; no one in this country has. I have only made it once in my life, and perhaps today in central Europe there still lives, in whatever vegetable ruin, the young man who saw it. He would be, now, about your age. Hopelessly insane. His name was Zvi. Will you tell the 'police,' or whatever they are calling themselves tonight, that I can make that face again? That it has an effective radius of a hundred yards and drives anyone unlucky enough to see it down forever into the darkened oubliette, among the terrible shapes, and secures the hatch irrevocably above them? Thank you."

The sirens had reached the front of the clinic. She heard car doors slamming, cops yelling, suddenly a great smash as they broke in. The office door opened then. Hilarius grabbed her by the wrist, pulled her inside, locked the door again.

"So now I'm a hostage," Oedipa said.

"Oh," said Hilarius, "it's you."

"Well who did you think you'd been—"

"Discussing my case with? Another. There is me, there are the others. You know, with the LSD, we're finding, the distinction begins to vanish. Egos lose their sharp edges. But I never took the drug, I chose to remain in relative paranoia, where at least I know who I am and who the others are. Perhaps that is why you also refused to participate, Mrs. Maas?" He held the rifle at sling arms and beamed at her. "Well, then. You were supposed to deliver a message to me, I assume. From them. What were you supposed to say?"

Oedipa shrugged. "Face up to your social responsibilities," she suggested. "Accept the reality principle. You're outnumbered and they have superior firepower."

"Ah, outnumbered. We were outnumbered there too." He watched her with a coy look.

"Where?"

"Where I made that face. Where I did my internship."

She knew then approximately what he was talking about, but to narrow it said, "Where," again.

"Buchenwald," replied Hilarius. Cops began hammering on the office door.

"He has a gun," Oedipa called, "and I'm in here."

"Who are you, lady?" She told him. "How do you spell that first name?" He also took down her address, age, phone number, next of kin, husband's occupation, for the news media. Hilarius all the while was rummaging in his desk for more ammo. "Can you talk him out of it?" the cop wanted to know. "TV folks would like to get some footage through the window. Could you keep him occupied?"

"Hang tough," Oedipa advised, "we'll see."

"Nice act you all have there," nodded Hilarius.

"You think," said Oedipa, "then, that they're trying to bring you back to Israel, to stand trial, like they did Eichmann?" The shrink kept nodding. "Why? What did you do at Buchenwald?"

"I worked," Hilarius told her, "on experimentally-induced insanity. A catatonic Jew was as good as a dead one. Liberal SS circles felt it would be more humane." So they had gone at their subjects with metronomes, serpents, Brechtian vignettes at midnight, surgical removal of certain glands, magic-lantern hallucinations, new drugs, threats recited over hidden loudspeakers, hypnotism, clocks that ran backward, and faces. Hilarius had been put in charge of faces. "The Allied liberators," he reminisced, "arrived, unfortunately, before we could gather enough data. Apart from the spectacular successes, like Zvi, there wasn't much we could point to in a statistical way." He smiled at the expression on her face. "Yes, you hate me. But didn't I try to atone? If I'd been a real Nazi I'd have chosen Jung, nicht wahr? But I chose Freud instead, the Jew. Freud's vision of the world had no Buchenwalds in it. Buchenwald, according to Freud, once the light was let in, would become a soccer field, fat children would learn flower-arranging and solfeggio in the strangling rooms. At Auschwitz the ovens would be converted over to petit fours and wedding cakes, and the V-2 missiles to public housing for the elves. I tried to believe it all. I slept three hours a night trying not to dream, and spent the other 21 at the forcible acquisition of faith. And yet my penance hasn't been enough. They've come like angels of death to get me, despite all I tried to do."

"How's it going?" the cop inquired.

"Just marv," said Oedipa. "I'll let you know if it's hopeless." Then she saw that Hilarius had left the Gewehr on his desk and was across the room ostensibly trying to open a file cabinet. She picked the rifle up, pointed it at him, and said, "I ought to kill you." She knew he had wanted her to get the weapon.

"Isn't that what you've been sent to do?" He crossed and uncrossed his eyes at her; stuck out his tongue tentatively.

"I came," she said, "hoping you could talk me out of a fantasy."

"Cherish it!" cried Hilarius, fiercely. "What else do any of you have? Hold it tightly by its little tentacle, don't let the Freudians coax it away or the pharmacists poison it out of you. Whatever it is, hold it dear, for when you lose it you go over by that much to the others. You begin to cease to be."

"Come on in," Oedipa yelled.

Tears sprang to Hilarius's eyes. "You aren't going to shoot?"

The cop tried the door. "It's locked, hey," he said.

"Bust it down," roared Oedipa, "and Hitler Hilarius here will foot the bill."

Outside, as a number of nervous patrolmen approached Hilarius, holding up strait jackets and billy clubs they would not need, and as three rival ambulances backed snarling up onto the lawn, jockeying for position, causing Helga Blamm between sobs to call the drivers filthy names, Oedipa spotted among searchlights and staring crowds a KCUF mobile unit, with her husband Mucho inside it, spieling into a microphone. She moseyed over past snapping flashbulbs and stuck her head in the window. "Hi."

Mucho pressed his cough button a moment, but only smiled. It seemed odd. How could they hear a smile? Oedipa got in, trying not to make noise. Mucho thrust the mike in front of her, mumbling, "You're on, just be yourself." Then in his earnest broadcasting voice, "How do you feel about this terrible thing?"

"Terrible," said Oedipa.

"Wonderful," said Mucho. He had her go on to give listeners a summary of what'd happened in the office. "Thank you, Mrs Edna Mosh," he wrapped up, "for your eyewitness account of this dramatic siege at the Hilarius Psychiatric Clinic. This is KCUF Mobile Two, sending it back now to 'Rabbit' Warren, at the studio." He cut his power. Something was not quite right.

"Edna Mosh?" Oedipa said.

"It'll come out the right way," Mucho said. "I was allowing for the distortion on these rigs, and then when they put it on tape."

"Where are they taking him?"

"Community hospital, I guess," Mucho said, "for observation. I wonder what they can observe."

"Israelis," Oedipa said, "coming in the windows. If there aren't any, he's crazy." Cops came over and they chatted awhile. They told her to stay around Kinneret in case there was legal action. At length she returned to her rented car and followed Mucho back to the studio. Tonight he had the one-to-six shift on the air.

In the hallway outside the loud ratcheting teletype room, Mucho upstairs in the office typing out his story, Oedipa encountered the program director, Caesar Funch. "Sure glad you're back," he greeted her, clearly at a loss for her first name.

"Oh?" said Oedipa, "and why is that."

"Frankly," confided Funch, "since you left, Wendell hasn't been himself."

"And who," said Oedipa, working herself into a rage because Funch was right, "pray, has he been, Ringo Starr?" Funch cowered. "Chubby Checker?" she pursued him toward the lobby, "the Righteous Brothers? And why tell me?"

"All of the above," said Funch, seeking to hide his head, "Mrs Maas."

"Oh, call me Edna. What do you mean?"

"Behind his back," Funch was whining, "they're calling him the Brothers N. He's losing his identity, Edna, how else can I put it? Day by day, Wendell is less himself and more generic. He enters a staff meeting and the room is suddenly full of people, you know? He's a walking assembly of man."

"It's your imagination," Oedipa said. "You've been smoking those cigarettes without the printing on them again."

"You'll see. Don't mock me. We have to stick together. Who else worries about him?"

She sat alone then on a bench outside Studio A, listening to Mucho's colleague Rabbit Warren spin records. Mucho came downstairs carrying his copy, a serenity about him she'd never seen. He used to hunch his shoulders and have a rapid eyeblink rate, and both now were gone. "Wait," he smiled, and dwindled down the hall. She scrutinized him from behind, trying to see iridescences, auras.

They had some time before he was on. They drove downtown to a pizzeria and bar, and faced each other through the fluted gold lens of a beer pitcher.

"How are you getting on with Metzger?" he said.

"There's nothing," she said.

"Not any more, at least," said Mucho. "I could tell that when you were talking into the mike."

"That's pretty good," Oedipa said. She couldn't figure the expression on his face.

"It's extraordinary," said Mucho, "everything's been—wait. Listen." She heard nothing unusual. "There are seventeen violins on that cut," Mucho said, "and one of them—I can't tell where he was because it's monaural here, damn." It dawned on her that he was talking about the Muzak. It has been seeping in, in its subliminal, unidentifiable way since they'd entered the place, all strings, reeds, muted brass.

"What is it," she said, feeling anxious.

"His E string," Mucho said, "it's a few cycles sharp. He can't be a studio musician. Do you think somebody could do the dinosaur bone bit with that one string, Oed? With just his set of notes on that cut. Figure out what his ear is like, and then the musculature of his hands and arms, and eventually the entire man. God, wouldn't that be wonderful."

"Why should you want to?"

"He was real. That wasn't synthetic. They could dispense with live musicians if they wanted. Put together all the right overtones at the right power levels so it'd come out like a violin. Like I . . ." he hesitated before breaking into a radiant smile, "you'll think I'm crazy, Oed. But I can do the same thing in reverse. Listen to anything and take it apart again. Spectrum analysis, in my head. I can break down chords, and timbres, and words too into all the basic frequencies and harmonics, with all their different loudnesses, and listen to them, each pure tone, but all at once."

"How can you do that?"

"It's like I have a separate channel for each one," Mucho said, excited, "and if I need more I just expand. Add on what I need. I don't know how it works, but lately I can do it with people talking too. Say 'rich, chocolaty goodness.' "

"Rich, chocolaty, goodness," said Oedipa.

"Yes," said Mucho, and fell silent.

"Well, *what?*" Oedipa asked after a couple minutes, with an edge to her voice.

"I noticed it the other night hearing Rabbit do a commercial. No matter who's talking, the different power spectra are the same, give or take a small percentage. So you and Rabbit have something in common now. More than that. Everybody who says the same words is the same person if the spectra are the same only they happen differently in time, you dig? But the time is arbitrary. You pick your zero point anywhere you want, that way you can shuffle each person's time line sideways till they all coincide. Then you'd have this big, God, maybe a couple hundred million chorus saying 'rich, chocolaty goodness' together, and it would all be the same voice."

"Mucho," she said, impatient but also flirting with a wild suspicion. "Is this what Funch means when he says you're coming on like a whole roomful of people?"

"That's what I am," said Mucho, "right. Everybody is." He gazed at her, perhaps having had his vision of consensus as others do orgasms, face now smooth, amiable, at peace. She didn't know him. Panic started to climb out of a dark region in her head. "Whenever I put the headset on now," he'd continued, "I really do understand what I find there. When those kids sing about 'She loves you,' yeah well, you know, she does, she's any number of people, all over the world, back through time, different colors, sizes, ages, shapes, distances from death, but she loves. And the 'you' is everybody. And herself. Oedipa, the human voice, you know, it's a flipping miracle." His eyes brimming, reflecting the color of beer.

"Baby," she said, helpless, knowing of nothing she could do for this, and afraid for him.

He put a little clear plastic bottle on the table between them. She stared at the pills in it, and then understood. "That's LSD?" she said. Mucho smiled back. "Where'd you get it?" Knowing.

"Hilarius. He broadened his program to include husbands."

"Look then," Oedipa said, trying to be businesslike, "how long has it been, that you've been on this?"

He honestly couldn't remember.

"But there may be a chance you're not addicted yet."

"Oed," looking at her puzzled, "you don't get addicted. It's not like you're some hophead. You take it because it's good. Because you hear and see things, even smell them, taste like you never could. Because the world is so abundant. No end to it, baby. You're an antenna, sending your pattern out across a million lives a night, and they're your lives too." He had this patient, motherly look now. Oedipa wanted to hit him in the mouth. "The songs, it's not just that they say something, they *are* something, in the pure sound. Something new. And my dreams have changed."

"Oh, goodo." Flipping her hair a couple times, furious, "No nightmares any more? Fine. So your latest little friend, whoever she is, she really made out. At that age, you know, they need all the sleep they can get."

"There's no girl, Oed. Let me tell you. The bad dream that I used to have all the time, about the car lot, remember that? I could never even tell you about it. But I can now. It doesn't bother me any more. It was only that sign in the lot, that's what scared me. In the dream I'd be going about a normal day's business and suddenly, with no warning, there'd be the sign. We were a member of the National Automobile Dealers' Association. N.A.D.A. Just this creaking metal sign that said nada, nada, against the blue sky. I used to wake up hollering."

She remembered. Now he would never be spooked again, not as long as he had the pills. She could not quite get it into her head that the day she'd left him for San Narciso was the day she'd seen Mucho for the last time. So much of him already had dissipated.

"Oh, listen," he was saying, "Oed, dig." But she couldn't even tell what the tune was.

When it was time for him to go back to the station, he nodded toward the pills. "You could have those."

She shook her head no.

"You're going back to San Narciso?"

"Tonight, yes."

"But the cops."

"I'll be a fugitive." Later she couldn't remember if they'd said anything else. At the station they kissed goodbye, all of them. As Mucho walked away he was whistling something complicated, twelve-tone. Oedipa sat with her forehead resting on the steering wheel and remembered that she hadn't asked him about the Trystero cancellation on his letter. But by then it was too late to make any difference.

6

When she got back to Echo Courts, she found Miles, Dean, Serge and Leonard arranged around and on the diving board at the end of the swimming pool with all their instruments, so composed and motionless that some photographer, hidden from Oedipa, might have been shooting them for an album illustration.

"What's happening?" said Oedipa.

"Your young man," replied Miles, "Metzger, really put it to Serge, our counter-tenor. The lad is crackers with grief."

"He's right, missus," said Serge. "I even wrote a song about it, whose arrangement features none other than me, and it goes like this."

SERGE'S SONG

> *What chance has a lonely surfer boy*
> *For the love of a surfer chick,*
> *With all these Humbert Humbert cats*
> *Coming on so big and sick?*
> *For me, my baby was a woman,*
> *For him she's just another nymphet;*

Why did they run around, why did she put me down,
And get me so upset?
Well, as long as she's gone away-yay,
I've had to find somebody new,
And the older generation
Has taught me what to do—
I had a date last night with an eight-year-old,
And she's a swinger just like me,
So you can find us any night up on the football field,
In back of P.S. 33 (oh, yeah),
And it's as groovy as it can be.

"You're trying to tell me something," said Oedipa.

They gave it to her then in prose. Metzger and Serge's chick had run off to Nevada, to get married. Serge, on close questioning, admitted the bit about the eight-year-old was so far only imaginary, but that he was hanging diligently around playgrounds and should have some news for them any day. On top of the TV set in her room Metzger had left a note telling her not to worry about the estate, that he'd turned over his executorship to somebody at Warpe, Wistfull, Kubitschek and McMingus, and they should be in touch with her, and it was all squared with the probate court also. No word to recall that Oedipa and Metzger had ever been more than co-executors.

Which must mean, thought Oedipa, that that's all we were. She should have felt more classically scorned, but had other things on her mind. First thing after unpacking she was on the horn to Randolph Driblette, the director. After about ten rings an elderly lady answered. "I'm sorry, we've nothing to say."

"Well who's this," Oedipa said.

Sigh. "This is his mother. There'll be a statement at noon tomorrow. Our lawyer will read it." She hung up. Now what the hell, Oedipa wondered: what had happened to Driblette? She decided to call later. She found Professor Emory Bortz's number in the book and had better luck. A wife named Grace answered, backed by a group of children. "He's pouring a patio," she told Oedipa. "It's a highly organized joke that's been going on since about April. He sits in the sun, drinks beer with students, lobs beer bottles at seagulls. You'd better talk to him before it gets that far. Maxine, why don't you throw that at your brother, he's more mobile than I am. Did you know Emory's done a new edition of Wharfinger? It'll be out——" but the date was obliterated by a great crash, maniacal childish laughter, high-pitched squeals. "Oh, God. Have you ever met an infanticide? Come on over, it may be your only chance."

Oedipa showered, put on a sweater, skirt and sneakers, wrapped her hair in a student like twist, went easy on the makeup. Recognizing with a vague sense of dread that it was not a matter of Bortz's response, or Grace's, but of The Trystero's.

Driving over she passed by Zapf's Used Books, and was alarmed to find a pile of charred rubble where the bookstore only a week ago had stood. There was still the smell of burnt leather. She stopped and went into the government surplus outlet next door. The owner informed her that Zapf, the damn fool, has set fire to his own store for the insurance. "Any kind of a wind," snarled this worthy, "it would have taken me with it. They only put up this complex here to last five years anyway. But could Zapf wait? Books." You had the feeling that it was only his good upbringing kept him from spitting. "You want to sell something used," he advised Oedipa, "find out what there's a demand for. This season now it's your rifles. Fella was in just this forenoon, bought two hundred for his drill team. I could've sold him two hundred of the swastika armbands too, only I was short, dammit."

"Government surplus swastikas?" Oedipa said.

"Hell no." He gave her an insider's wink. "Got this little factory down outside of San Diego," he told her, "got a dozen of your niggers, say, they can sure turn them old armbands out. You'd be amazed how that little number's selling. I took some space in a couple of the girlie magazines, and I had to hire two extra niggers last week just to take care of the mail."

"What's your name?" Oedipa said.

"Winthrop Tremaine," replied the spirited entrepreneur, "Winner, for short. Listen, now we're getting up an arrangement with one of the big ready-to-wear outfits in L.A. to see how SS uniforms go for the fall. We're working it in with the back-to-school campaign, lot of 37 longs, you know, teenage kid sizes. Next season we may go all the way and get out a modified version for the ladies. How would that strike you?"

"I'll let you know," Oedipa said. "I'll keep you in mind." She left, wondering if she should've called him something, or tried to hit him with any of a dozen surplus, heavy, blunt objects in easy reach. There had been no witnesses. Why hadn't she?

You're chicken, she told herself, snapping her seat belt. This is America, you live in it, you let it happen. Let it unfurl. She drove savagely along the freeway, hunting for Volkswagens. By the time she'd pulled into Bortz's subdivision, a riparian settlement in the style of Fangoso Lagoons, she was only shaking and a little nauseous in the stomach.

She was greeted by a small fat girl with some blue substance smeared all over her face. "Hi," said Oedipa, "you must be Maxine."

"Maxine's in bed. She threw one of Daddy's beer bottles at Charles and it went through the window and Mama spanked her good. If she was mine I'd drown her."

"Never thought of doing it that way," said Grace Bortz, materializing from the dim living room. "Come on in." With a wet washcloth she started to clean off her child's face. "How did you manage to get away from yours today?"

"I don't have any," said Oedipa, following her into the kitchen.

Grace looked surprised. "There's a certain harassed style," she said, "you get to recognize. I thought only kids caused it. I guess not."

Emory Bortz lay half in a hammock, surrounded by three graduate students, two male, one female, all sodden with drink, and an astounding accumulation of empty beer bottles. Oedipa located a full one and seated herself on the grass. "I would like to find out," she presently plunged, "something about the historical Wharfinger. Not so much the verbal one."

"The historical Shakespeare," growled one of the grad students through a full beard, uncapping another bottle. "The historical Marx. The historical Jesus."

"He's right," shrugged Bortz, "they're dead. What's left?"

"Words."

"Pick some words," said Bortz. "Them, we can talk about."

" 'No hallowed skein of stars can ward, I trow,' " quoted Oedipa, " 'Who's once been set his tryst with Trystero.' *Courier's Tragedy,* Act IV, Scene 8."

Bortz blinked at her. "And how," he said, "did you get into the Vatican library?"

Oedipa showed him the paperback with the line in it. Bortz, squinting at the page, groped for another beer. "My God," he announced, "I've been pirated, me and Wharfinger, we've been Bowdlerized in reverse or something." He flipped to the front, to see who'd re-edited his edition of Wharfinger. "Ashamed to sign it. Damn. I'll have to write the publishers. K. da Chingado and Company? You ever heard of them? New York." He looked at the sun through a page or two. "Offset." Brought his nose close to the text. "Misprints. Gah. Corrupt." He dropped the book on the grass and looked at it with loathing. "How did *they* get into the Vatican, then?"

"What's in the Vatican?" asked Oedipa.

"A pornographic *Courier's Tragedy*. I didn't get to see it till '61, or I would've given it a note in my old edition."

"What I saw out at the Tank Theatre wasn't pornographic?"

"Randy Driblette's production? No, I thought it was typically virtuous." He looked sadly past her toward a stretch of sky. "He was a peculiarly moral man. He felt hardly any responsibility toward the word, really; but to the invisible field surrounding the play, its spirit, he was always intensely faithful. If anyone could have called up for you that historical Wharfinger you want, it'd've been Randy. Nobody else I ever knew was so close to the author, to the microcosm of that play as it must have surrounded Wharfinger's living mind."

"But you're using the past tense," Oedipa said, her heart pounding, remembering the old lady on the phone.

"Hadn't you heard?" They all looked at her. Death glided by, shadowless, among the empties on the grass.

"Randy walked into the Pacific two nights ago," the girl told her finally. Her eyes had been red all along. "In his Gennaro suit. He's dead, and this is a wake."

"I tried to call him this morning," was all Oedipa could think of to say.

"It was right after they struck the set of *The Courier's Tragedy*," Bortz said.

Even a month ago, Oedipa's next question would have been, "Why?" But now she kept a silence, waiting, as if to be illuminated.

They are stripping from me, she said subvocally—feeling like a fluttering curtain in a very high window, moving up to then out over the abyss—they are stripping away, one by one, my men. My shrink, pursued by Israelis, has gone mad; my husband, on LSD, gropes like a child further and further into the rooms and endless rooms of the elaborate candy house of himself and away, hopelessly away, from what has passed, I was hoping forever, for love; my one extra-marital fella has eloped with a depraved 15-year-old; my best guide back to the Trystero has taken a Brody. Where am I?

"I'm sorry," Bortz had also said, watching her.

Oedipa stayed with it. "Did he use only that," pointing to the paperback, "for his script?"

"No." Frowning. "He used the hardcover, my edition."

"But the night you saw the play." Too much sunlight shone on the bottles, silent all around them. "How did he end the fourth act? What were his lines, Driblette's, Gennaro's, when they're all standing around at the lake, after the miracle?"

" 'He that we last as Thurn and Taxis knew,' " recited Bortz, " 'Now recks no lord but the stiletto's Thorn,/And Tacit lies the gold once-knotted horn.' "

"Right," agreed the grad students, "yeah."

"That's all? What about the rest? The other couplet?"

"In the text I go along with personally," said Bortz, "that other couplet has the last line suppressed. The book in the Vatican is only an obscene parody. The ending 'Who once has crossed the lusts of Angelo' was put in by the printer of the 1687 Quarto. The 'Whitechapel' version is corrupt. So Randy did the best thing—left the doubtful part out altogether."

"But the night I was there," said Oedipa, "Driblette did use the Vatican lines, he said the word Trystero."

Bortz's face stayed neutral. "It was up to him. He was both director and actor, right?"

"But would it be just," she gestured in circles with her hands, "just some whim? To use another couple lines like that, without telling anybody?"

"Randy," recalled the third grad student, a stocky kid with hornrims, "what was bugging him inside, usually, somehow or other, would have to come outside, on stage. He might have looked at a lot of versions, to develop a feel for the spirit of the play, not necessarily the words, and that's how he came across your paperback there, with the variation in it."

"Then," Oedipa concluded, "something must have happened in his personal life, something must have changed for him drastically that night, and that's what made him put the lines in."

"Maybe," said Bortz, "maybe not. You think a man's mind is a pool table?"

"I hope not."

"Come in and see some dirty pictures," Bortz invited, rolling off the hammock. They left the students drinking beer. "Illicit microfilms of the illustrations in that Vatican edition. Smuggled out in '61. Grace and I were there on a grant."

They entered a combination workroom and study. Far away in the house children screamed, a vacuum whined. Bortz drew shades, riffled through a box of slides, selected a handful, switched on a projector and aimed it at a wall.

The illustrations were woodcuts, executed with that crude haste to see the finished product that marks the amateur. True pornography is given us by vastly patient professionals.

"The artist is anonymous," Bortz said, "so is the poetaster who rewrote the play. Here Pasquale, remember, one of the bad guys? actually does marry his mother, and there's a whole scene on their wedding night." He changed slides. "You get the general idea. notice how often the figure of Death hovers in the background. The moral rage, it's a throwback, it's mediaeval. No Puritan ever got that violent. Except possibly the Scurvhamites. D'Amico thinks this edition was a Scurvhamite project."

"Scurvhamite?"

Robert Scurvham had founded, during the reign of Charles I, a sect of most pure Puritans. Their central hangup had to do with predestination. There were two kinds. Nothing for a Scurvhamite ever happened by accident, Creation was a vast, intricate machine. But one part of it, the Scurvhamite part, ran off the will of God, its prime mover. The rest ran off some opposite Principle, something blind, soulless; a brute automatism that led to eternal death. The idea was to woo converts into the Godly and purposeful sodality of the Scurvhamite. But somehow those few saved Scurvhamites found themselves looking out into the gaudy clockwork of the doomed with a certain sick and fascinated horror, and this was to prove fatal. One by one the glamorous prospect of annihilation coaxed them over, until there was no one left in the sect, not even Robert Scurvham, who, like a ship's master, had been last to go.

"What did Richard Wharfinger have to do with them?" asked Oedipa. "Why should they do a dirty version of his play?"

"As a moral example. They were not fond of the theater. It was their way of putting the play entirely away from them, into hell. What better way to damn it eternally than to change the actual words. Remember that Puritans were utterly devoted, like literary critics, to the Word."

"But the line about Trystero isn't dirty."

He scratched his head. "It fits, surely? The 'hallowed skein of stars' is God's will. But even that can't ward, or guard, somebody who has an appointment with Trystero. I mean, say you only talked about crossing the lusts of Angelo, hell, there'd be any number of ways to get out of that. Leave the country. Angelo's only a man. But the brute Other, that kept the nonScurvhamite universe running like clockwork, that was something else again. Evidently they felt Trystero would symbolize the Other quite well."

She had nothing more then to put it off with. Again with the light, vertiginous sense of fluttering out over an abyss, she asked what she'd come there to ask. "What was Trystero?"

"One of several brand new areas," said Bortz, "that opened up after I did that edition in '57. We've since come across some interesting old source material. My updated edition ought to be out, they tell me, next year sometime. Meanwhile." He went looking in a glass case full of ancient books. "Here," producing one with a dark brown, peeling calf cover. "I keep my Wharfingeriana locked in here so the kids can't get at it. Charles could ask no end of questions I'm too young to cope with yet." The book was titled *An Account of the Singular Peregrinations of Dr. Diocletian Blobb among the Italians, Illuminated with Exemplary Tales from the True History of That Outlandish And Fantastical Race.*

"Lucky for me," said Bortz, "Wharfinger, like Milton, kept a commonplace book, where he jotted down quotes and things from his reading. That's how we know about Blobb's *Peregrinations.*"

It was full of words ending in e's, s's that looked like f's, capitalized nouns, y's where i's should've been. "I can't read this," Oedipa said.

"Try," said Bortz. "I have to see those kids off. I think it's around Chapter Seven." And disappeared, to leave Oedipa before the tabernacle. As it turned out it was Chapter Eight she wanted, a report of the author's own encounter with the Trystero brigands. Diocletian Blobb had chosen to traverse a stretch of desolate mountain country in a mail coach belonging to the "Torre and Tassis" system, which Oedipa figured must be Italian for Thurn and Taxis. Without warning, by the shores of what Blobb called "the Lake of Piety," they were set upon by a score of black-cloaked riders, who engaged them in a fierce, silent struggle in the icy wind blowing in from the lake. The marauders used cudgels, harquebuses, swords, stilettos, at the end silk kerchiefs to dispatch those still breathing. All except for Dr. Blobb and his servant, who had dissociated themselves from the hassle at the very outset, proclaimed in loud voices that they were British subjects, and even from time to time "ventured to sing certain of the more improving of our Church hymns." Their escape surprised Oedipa, in view of what seemed to be Trystero's passion for security.

"Was Trystero trying to set up shop in England?" Bortz suggested, days later.

Oedipa didn't know. "But why spare an insufferable ass like Diocletian Blobb?"

"You can spot a mouth like that a mile off," Bortz said. "Even in the cold, even with your blood-lust up. If I wanted word to get to England, to sort of pave the way, I should think he'd be perfect. Trystero enjoyed counter-revolution in those days. Look at England, the king about to lose his head. A set-up."

The leader of the brigands, after collecting the mail sacks, had pulled Blobb from the coach and addressed him in perfect English: "Messer, you have witnessed the wrath of Trystero. Know that we are not without mercy. Tell your king and Parliament what we have done. Tell them that we prevail. That neither tempest nor strife, nor fierce beasts, nor the loneliness of the desert, nor yet the illegitimate usurpers of our rightful estate, can deter our couriers." And leaving them and their purses intact, the highwaymen, in a cracking of cloaks like black sails, vanished back into their twilit mountains.

Blobb inquired around about the Trystero organization, running into zipped mouths nearly every way he turned. But he was able to collect a few fragments. So, in the days following, was Oedipa. From obscure philatelic journals furnished her by Genghis Cohen, an ambiguous footnote in Motley's *Rise of the Dutch Republic,* an 80-year-old pamphlet on the roots of modern anarchism, a book of sermons by Blobb's brother Augustine also among Bortz's Wharfingeriana, along with Blobb's original clues, Oedipa was able to fit together this account of how the organization began:

In 1577, the northern provinces of the Low Countries, led by the Protestant noble William of Orange, had been struggling nine years for independence from Catholic Spain and a Catholic Holy Roman Emperor. In late December, Orange, de facto master of the Low Countries, entered Brussels in triumph, having been invited there by a Committee of Eighteen. This was a junta of Calvinist fanatics who felt that the Estates-General, controlled by the privileged classes, no longer represented the skilled workers, had lost touch entirely with the people. The Committee set up a kind of Brussels Commune. They controlled the police, dictated all decisions of the Estates-General, and threw out many holders of high position in Brussels. Among these was Leonard I, Baron of Taxis, Gentleman of the Emperor's Privy Chamber and Baron of Buysinghen, the hereditary Grand Master of the Post for the Low Countries, and executor of the Thurn and Taxis monopoly. He was replaced by one Jan Hinckart, Lord of Ohain, a loyal adherent of Orange. At this point the founding figure enters the scene: Hernando Joaquín de Tristero y Calavera, perhaps a madman, perhaps an honest rebel, according to some only a con artist. Tristero claimed to be Jan Hinckart's cousin, from the Spanish and legitimate branch of the family, and true lord of Ohain—rightful heir to everything Jan Hinckart then possessed, including his recent appointment as Grand Master.

From 1578 until Alexander Farnese took Brussels back again for the Emperor in March, 1585, Tristero kept up what amounted to a guerrilla war against his cousin—if Hinckart was his cousin. Being Spanish, he got little support. Most of the time, from one quarter or another, his life was in danger. Still, he tried four times to assassinate Orange's postmaster, though without success.

Jan Hinckart was dispossessed by Farnese, and Leonard I, the Thurn and Taxis Grand Master, reinstated. But it had been a time of great instability for the Thurn and Taxis monopoly. Leery of strong Protestant leanings in the Bohemian branch of the family, the Emperor, Rudolph II, had for a time withdrawn his patronage. The postal operation plunged deeply into the red.

It may have been some vision of the continent-wide power structure Hinckart could have taken over, now momentarily weakened and tottering, that inspired Tristero to set up his own system. He seems to have been highly unstable, apt at any time to appear at a public function and begin a speech. His constant theme, disinheritance. The postal monopoly belonged to Ohain by right of conquest, and Ohain belonged to Tristero by right of blood. He styled himself El Desheredado, The Disinherited, and fashioned a livery of black for his followers, black to symbolize the only thing that truly belonged to them in their exile: the night. Soon he had added to his iconography the muted post horn and a dead badger with its four feet in the air (some said that the name Taxis came from the Italian *tasso,* badger, referring to hats of badger fur the early Bergamascan couriers wore). He began a sub rosa campaign of obstruction, terror and depredation along the Thurn and Taxis mail routes.

Oedipa spent the next several days in and out of libraries and earnest discussions with Emory Bortz and Genghis Cohen. She feared a little for their security in view of what was happening to everyone else she knew. The day after reading Blobb's *Peregrinations* she, with Bortz, Grace, and the graduate students, attended Randolph Driblette's burial, listened to a younger brother's helpless, stricken eulogy, watched the mother, spectral in afternoon smog, cry, and came back at night to sit on the grave and drink

Napa Valley muscatel, which Driblette in his time had put away barrels of. There was no moon, smog covered the stars, all black as a Tristero rider. Oedipa sat on the earth, ass getting cold, wondering whether, as Driblette had suggested that night from the shower, some version of herself hadn't vanished with him. Perhaps her mind would go on flexing psychic muscles that no longer existed; would be betrayed and mocked by a phantom self as the amputee is by a phantom limb. Someday she might replace whatever of her had gone away by some prosthetic device, a dress of a certain color, a phrase in a letter, another lover. She tried to reach out, to whatever coded tenacity of protein might improbably have held on six feet below, still resisting decay—any stubborn quiescence perhaps gathering itself for some last burst, some last scramble up through earth, just-glimmering, holding together with its final strength a transient, winged shape, needing to settle at once in the warm host, or dissipate forever into the dark. If you come to me, prayed Oedipa, bring your memories of the last night. Or if you have to keep down your payload, the last five minutes—that may be enough. But so I'll know if your walk into the sea had anything to do with Tristero. If they got rid of you for the reason they got rid of Hilarius and Mucho and Metzger—maybe because they thought I no longer needed you. They were wrong. I needed you. Only bring me that memory, and you can live with me for whatever time I've got. She remembered his head, floating in the shower, saying, you could fall in love with me. But could she have saved him? She looked over at the girl who'd given her the news of his death. Had they been in love? Did she know why Driblette had put in those two extra lines that night? Had *he* even known why? No one could begin to trace it. A hundred hangups, permuted, combined—sex, money, illness, despair with the history of his time and place, who knew. Changing the script had no clearer motive than his suicide. There was the same whimsy to both. Perhaps—she felt briefly penetrated, as if the bright winged thing had actually made it to the sanctuary of her heart—perhaps, springing from the same slick labyrinth, adding those two lines had even, in a way never to be explained, served him as a rehearsal for his night's walk away into that vast sink of the primal blood the Pacific. She waited for the winged brightness to announce its safe arrival. But there was silence. Driblette, she called. The signal echoing down twisted miles of brain circuitry. Driblette!

But as with Maxwell's Demon, so now. Either she could not communicate, or he did not exist.

Beyond its origins, the libraries told her nothing more about Tristero. For all they knew, it had never survived the struggle for Dutch independence. To find the rest, she had to approach from the Thurn and Taxis side. This had its perils. For Emory Bortz it seemed to turn into a species of cute game. He held, for instance, to a mirror-image theory, by which any period of instability for Thurn and Taxis must have its reflection in Tristero's shadow-state. He applied this to the mystery of why the dread name should have appeared in print only around the middle of the 17th century. How had the author of the pun on "this Trystero *dies irae*" overcome his reluctance? How had half the Vatican couplet, with its suppression of the "Trystero" line, found its way into the Folio? Whence had the daring of even hinting at a Thurn and Taxis rival come? Bortz maintained there must have been some crisis inside Tristero grave enough to keep them from retaliating. Perhaps the same that kept them from taking the life of Dr Blobb.

But should Bortz have exfoliated the mere words so lushly, into such unnatural roses, under which, in whose red, scented dusk, dark history slithered unseen? When Leonard II-Francis, Count of Thurn and Taxis, died in 1628, his wife Alexandrine of Rye succeeded him in name as postmaster, though her tenure was never considered official. She retired in 1645. The actual locus of power in the monopoly remained uncertain until 1650, when the next male heir, Lamoral II-Claude-Francis, took over. Meanwhile, in Brussels and Antwerp signs of decay in the system had appeared. Private local posts had encroached so far on the Imperial licenses that the two cities shut down their Thurn and Taxis offices.

How, Bortz asked, would Tristero have responded? Postulating then some militant faction proclaiming the great moment finally at hand. Advocating a takeover by force, while their enemy was vulnerable. But conservative opinion would care only to continue in opposition, exactly as the Tristero had these seventy years. There might also be, say, a few visionaries: men above the immediacy of their time who could think historically. At least one among them hip enough to foresee the end of the Thirty Years' War, the Peace of Westphalia, the breakup of the Empire, the coming descent into particularism.

"He looks like Kirk Douglas," cried Bortz, "he's wearing this sword, his name is something gutsy like Konrad. They're meeting in the back room of a tavern, all these broads in peasant blouses carrying steins around, everybody juiced and yelling, suddenly Konrad jumps up on a table. The crowd hushes, 'The salvation of Europe,' Konrad says, 'depends on communication, right? We face this anarchy of jealous German princes, hundreds of them scheming, counterscheming, infighting, dissipating all of the Empire's strength in their useless bickering. But whoever could control the lines of communication, among all these princes, would control them. That network someday could unify the Continent. So I propose that we merge with our old enemy Thurn and Taxis——' Cries of no, never, throw the traitor out, till this barmaid, little starlet, sweet on Konrad, cold-conks with a stein his loudest antagonist. 'Together,' Konrad is saying, 'our two systems could be invincible. We could refuse service on any but an Imperial basis. Nobody could move troops, farm produce, anything, without us. Any prince tries to start his own courier system, we suppress it. We, who have so long been disinherited, could be the heirs of Europe!' Prolonged cheering."

"But they *didn't* keep the Empire from falling apart," Oedipa pointed out.

"So," Bortz backing off, "the militants and the conservatives fight to a standstill, Konrad and his little group of visionaries, being nice guys, try to mediate the hassle, by the time they all get squared away again, everybody's played out, the Empire's had it, Thurn and Taxis wants no deals."

And with the end of the Holy Roman Empire, the fountainhead of Thurn and Taxis legitimacy is lost forever among the other splendid delusions. Possibilities for paranoia become abundant. If Tristero has managed to maintain even partial secrecy, if Thurn and Taxis have no clear idea who their adversary is, or how far its influence extends, then many of them must come to believe in something very like the Scurvhamite's blind, automatic anti-God. Whatever it is, it has the power to murder their riders, send landslides thundering across their roads, by extension bring into being new local competition and presently even state postal monopolies; disintegrate their Empire. It is their time's ghost, out to put the Thurn and Taxis ass in a sling.

But over the next century and a half the paranoia recedes, as they come to discover the secular Tristero. Power, omniscience, implacable malice, attributes of what they'd thought to be a historical principle, a Zeitgeist, are carried over to the now human enemy. So much that, by 1795, it is even suggested that Tristero has staged the entire French Revolution, just for an excuse to issue the Proclamation of 9th Frimaire, An III, ratifying the end of the Thurn and Taxis postal monopoly in France and the Lowlands.

"Suggested by who, though," said Oedipa. "Did you read that someplace?"

"Wouldn't somebody have brought it up?" Bortz said. "Maybe not."

She didn't press the argument. Having begun to feel reluctant about following up anything. She hadn't asked Genghis Cohen, for example, if his Expert Committee had ever reported back on the stamps he'd sent them. She knew that if she went back to Vesperhaven House to talk again to old Mr Thoth about his grandfather, she would find that he too had died. She knew she ought to write to K. da Chingado, publisher of the unaccountable paperback *Courier's Tragedy,* but she didn't, and never asked Bortz if he had, either. Worst of all, she found herself going often to absurd lengths to avoid talking about Randolph Driblette. Whenever the girl showed up, the one who'd been at the wakes, Oedipa found excuses to leave the gathering. She felt she was betraying Driblette and herself. But left it alone, anxious that her revelation not expand beyond a certain point. Lest, possibly, it grow larger than she and assume her to itself. When Bortz asked her one evening if he could bring in D'Amico, who was at NYU, Oedipa told him no, too fast, too nervous. He didn't mention it again and neither, of course, did she.

She did go back to The Scope, though, one night, restless, alone, leery of what she might find. She found Mike Fallopian, a couple weeks into raising a beard, wearing button-down olive shirt, creased fatigue pants minus cuffs and belt loops, two-button fatigue jacket, no hat. He was surrounded by broads, drinking champagne cocktails, and bellowing low songs. When he spotted Oedipa he gave her the wide grin and waved her over.

"You look," she said, "wow. Like you're all on the move. Training rebels up in the mountains." Hostile looks from the girls twined around what parts of Fallopian were accessible.

"It's a revolutionary secret," he laughed, throwing up his arms and flinging off a couple of camp-followers. "Go on, now, all of you. I want to talk to this one." When they were out of earshot he swiveled on her a look sympathetic, annoyed, perhaps also a little erotic. "How's your quest?"

She gave him a quick status report. He kept quiet while she talked, his expression slowly changing to something she couldn't recognize. It bothered her. To jog him a little, she said, "I'm surprised you people aren't using the system too."

"Are we an underground?" he came back, mild enough. "Are we rejects?"

"I didn't mean——"

"Maybe we haven't found them yet," said Fallopian. "Or maybe they haven't approached us. Or maybe we are using W.A.S.T.E., only it's a secret." Then, as electronic music began to percolate into the room, "But there's another angle too." She sensed what he was going to say and began, reflexively, to grind together her back molars. A nervous habit she'd developed in the last few days. "Has it ever occurred to you, Oedipa, that somebody's putting you on? That this is all a hoax, maybe something Inverarity set up before he died?"

It had occurred to her. But like the thought that someday she would have to die, Oedipa had been steadfastly refusing to look at that possibility directly, or in any but the most accidental of lights. "No," she said, "that's ridiculous."

Fallopian watched her, nothing if not compassionate. "You ought," quietly, "really, you ought to think about it. Write down what you can't deny. Your hard intelligence. But then write down what you've only speculated, assumed. See what you've got. At least that."

"Go ahead," she said, cold, "at least that. What else, after that?"

He smiled, perhaps now trying to salvage whatever was going soundlessly smash, its net of invisible cracks propagating leisurely though the air between them. "Please don't be mad."

"Verify my sources, I suppose," Oedipa kept on, pleasantly. "Right?"

He didn't say any more.

She stood up, wondering if her hair was in place, if she looked rejected or hysterical, if they'd been causing a scene. "I knew you'd be different," she said, "Mike, because everybody's been changing on me. But it hadn't gone as far as hating me."

"Hating you." He shook his head and laughed.

"If you need any armbands or more weapons, do try Winthrop Tremaine, over by the freeway. Tremaine's Swastika Shoppe. Mention my name."

"We're already in touch, thanks." She left him, in his modified Cuban ensemble, watching the floor, waiting for his broads to come back.

Well, what about her sources? She was avoiding the question, yes. One day Genghis Cohen called, sounding excited, and asked her to come see something he'd just got in the mail, the U.S. Mail. It turned out to be an old American stamp, bearing the device of the muted post horn, belly-up badger, and the motto: WE AWAIT SILENT TRISTERO'S EMPIRE.

"So that's what it stands for," said Oedipa. "Where did you get this?"

"A friend," Cohen said, leafing through a battered Scott catalogue, "in San Francisco." As usual she did not go on to ask for any name or address. "Odd. He said he couldn't find the stamp listed. But here it is. An addendum, look." In the front of the book a slip of paper had been pasted in. The stamp, designated 163L1, was reproduced, under the title "Tristero Rapid Post, San Francisco, California," and should have been inserted between

Local listings 139 (the Third Avenue Post Office, of New York) and 140 (Union Post, also of New York). Oedipa, off on a kind of intuitive high, went immediately to the end-paper in back and found the sticker of Zapf's Used Books.

"Sure," Cohen protested. "I drove out there one day to see Mr Metzger, while you were up north. This is the Scott Specialized, you see, for American stamps, a catalogue I don't generally keep up on. My field being European and colonial. But my curiosity had been aroused, so——"

"Sure," Oedipa said. Anybody could paste in an addendum. She drove back to San Narciso to have another look at the list of Inverarity's assets. Sure enough, the whole shopping center that housed Zapf's Used Books and Tremaine's surplus place had been owned by Pierce. Not only that, but the Tank Theater, also.

OK, Oedipa told herself, stalking around the room, her viscera hollow, waiting on something truly terrible, OK. It's unavoidable, isn't it? Every access route to the Tristero could be traced also back to the Inverarity estate. Even Emory Bortz, with his copy of Blobb's *Peregrinations* (bought, she had no doubt he'd tell her in the event she asked, also at Zapf's), taught now at San Narciso College, heavily endowed by the dead man.

Meaning what? That Bortz, along with Metzger, Cohen, Driblette, Koteks, the tattooed sailor in San Francisco, the W.A.S.T.E. carriers she'd seen—that all of them were Pierce Inverarity's men? *Bought?* Or loyal, for free, for fun, to some grandiose practical joke he'd cooked up, all for her embarrassment, or terrorizing, or moral improvement?

Change your name to Miles, Dean, Serge, and /or Leonard, baby, she advised her reflection in the half-light of that afternoon's vanity mirror. Either way, they'll call it paranoia. They. Either you have stumbled indeed, without the aid of LSD or other indole alkaloids, onto a secret richness and concealed density of dream; onto a network by which X number of Americans are truly communicating whilst reserving their lies, recitations of routine, arid betrayals of spiritual poverty, for the official government delivery system; maybe even onto a real alternative to the exitlessness, to the absence of surprise to life, that harrows the head of everybody American you know, and you too, sweetie. Or you are hallucinating it. Or a plot has been mounted against you, so expensive and elaborate, involving items like the forging of stamps and ancient books, constant surveillance of your movements, planting of post horn images all over San Francisco, bribing of librarians, hiring of professional actors and Pierce Inverarity only knows what-all besides, all financed out of the estate in a way either too secret or too involved for your non-legal mind to know about even though you are co-executor, so labyrinthine that it must have meaning beyond just a practical joke. Or you are fantasying some such plot, in which case you are a nut, Oedipa, out of your skull.

Those, now that she was looking at them, she saw to be the alternatives. Those symmetrical four. She didn't like any of them, but hoped she was mentally ill; that that's all it was. That night she sat for hours, too numb even to drink, teaching herself to breathe in a vacuum. For this, oh God, was the void. There was nobody who could help her. Nobody in the world. They were all on something, mad, possible enemies, dead.

Old fillings in her teeth began to bother her. She would spend nights staring at a ceiling lit by the pink glow of San Narciso's sky. Other nights she could sleep for eighteen drugged hours and wake, enervated, hardly able to stand. In conferences with the keen, fast-talking old man who was new counsel for the estate, her attention span could often be measured in seconds, and she laughed nervously more than she spoke. Waves of nausea, lasting five to ten minutes, would strike her at random, cause her deep misery, then vanish as if they had never been. There were headaches, nightmares, menstrual pains. One day she drove into L.A., picked a doctor at random from the phone book, went to her, told her she thought she was pregnant. They arranged for tests. Oedipa gave her name as Grace Bortz and didn't show up for her next appointment.

Genghis Cohen, once so shy, now seemed to come up with new goodies every other day—a listing in an outdated Zumstein catalogue, a friend in the Royal Philatelic Society's dim memory of some muted post horn spied in the catalogue of an auction held at Dresden in 1923; one day a typescript, sent him by another friend in New York. It was supposed to be a translation of an article from an 1865 issue of the famous *Bibliothèque des Timbrophiles* of Jean-Baptiste Moens. Reading like another of Bortz's costume dramas, it told of a great schism in the Tristero ranks during the French Revolution. According to the recently discovered and decrypted journals of the Comte Raoul Antoine de Vouziers, Marquis de Tour et Tassis, one element among the Tristero had never accepted the passing of the Holy Roman Empire, and saw the Revolution as a temporary madness. Feeling obliged, as fellow aristocrats, to help Thurn and Taxis weather its troubles, they put out probes to see if the house was interested at all in being subsidized. This move split The Tristero wide open. At a convention held in Milan, arguments raged for a week, life-long enmities were created, families divided, blood spilt. At the end of it a resolution to subsidize Thurn and Taxis failed. Many conservatives, taking this as a Millennial judgment against them, ended their association with The Tristero. *Thus,* the article smugly concluded, *did the organization enter the penumbra of historical eclipse. From the battle of Austerlitz until the difficulties of 1848, the Tristero drifted on, deprived of nearly all the noble patronage that had sustained them; now reduced to handling anarchist correspondence;*

only peripherally engaged—in Germany with the ill-fated Frankfurt Assembly, in Buda-Pesth at the barricades, perhaps even among the watchmakers of the Jura, preparing them for the coming of M. Bakunin. By far the greatest number, however, fled to America during 1849–50, where they are no doubt at present rendering their services to those who seek to extinguish the flame of Revolution.

Less excited than she might have been even a week ago, Oedipa showed the piece to Emory Bortz. "All the Tristero refugees from the 1849 reaction arrive in America," it seemed to him, "full of high hopes. Only what do they find?" Not really asking; it was part of his game. "Trouble." Around 1845 the U. S. government had carried out a great postal reform, cutting their rates, putting most independent mail routes out of business. By the '70's and '80's, any independent carrier that tried to compete with the government was immediately squashed. 1849–50 was no time for any immigrating Tristero to get ideas about picking up where they'd left off back in Europe.

"So they simply stay on," Bortz said, "in the context of conspiracy. Other immigrants come to America looking for freedom from tyranny, acceptance by the culture, assimilation into it, this melting pot. Civil War comes along, most of them, being liberals, sign up to fight to preserve the Union. But clearly not the Tristero. All they've done is to change oppositions. By 1861 they're well established, not about to be suppressed. While the Pony Express is defying deserts, savages and sidewinders, Tristero's giving its employees crash courses in Siouan and Athapascan dialects. Disguised as Indians their messengers mosey westward. Reach the Coast every time, zero attrition rate, not a scratch on them. Their entire emphasis now toward silence, impersonation, opposition masquerading as allegiance."

"What about that stamp of Cohen's? We Await Silent Tristero's Empire."

"They were more open in their youth. Later, as the Feds cracked down, they went over to stamps that were almost kosher-looking, but not quite."

Oedipa knew them by heart. In the 15¢ dark green from the 1893 Columbian Exposition Issue ("Columbus Announcing His Discovery"), the faces of three courtiers, receiving the news at the right-hand side of the stamp, had been subtly altered to express uncontrollable fright. In the 3¢ Mothers of America Issue, put out on Mother's Day, 1934, the flowers to the lower left of Whistler's Mother had been replaced by Venus's-flytrap, belladonna, poison sumac and a few others Oedipa had never seen. In the 1947 Postage Stamp Centenary Issue, commemorating the great postal reform that had meant the beginning of the end for private carriers, the head of a Pony Express rider at the lower left was set at a disturbing angle unknown among the living. The deep violet 3¢ regular issue of 1954 had a faint, menacing smile on the face of the Statue of Liberty. The Brussels Exhibition Issue of 1958 included in its aerial view of the U. S. pavilion at Brussels, and set slightly off from the other tiny fairgoers, the unmistakable silhouette of a horse and rider. There were also the Pony Express stamp Cohen had showed her on her first visit, the Lincoln 4¢ with "U. S. Potsage," the sinister 8¢ airmail she'd seen on the tattooed sailor's letter in San Francisco.

"Well, it's interesting," she said, "if the article's legitimate."

"That ought to be easy enough to check out." Bortz gazing straight into her eyes. "Why don't you?"

The toothaches got worse, she dreamed of disembodied voices from whose malignance there was no appeal, the soft dusk of mirrors out of which something was about to walk, and empty rooms that waited for her. Your gynecologist has no test for what she was pregnant with.

One day Cohen called to tell her that the final arrangements had been made to auction off Inverarity's stamp collection. The Tristero "forgeries" were to be sold, as lot 49. "And something rather disturbing, Miz Maas. A new book bidder has appeared on the scene, whom neither I nor any of the firms in the area have heard of before. That hardly ever happens."

"A what?"

Cohen explained how there were floor bidders, who would attend the auction in person, and book bidders, who would send in their bids by mail. These bids would be entered in a special book by the auction firm, hence the name. There would be, as was customary, no public disclosure of persons for whom "the book" would be bidding.

"Then how do you know he's a stranger?"

"Word gets around. He's being super-secretive—working through an agent, C. Morris Schrift, a very reputable, good man. Morris was in touch with the auctioneers yesterday to tell them his client wanted to examine our forgeries, lot 49, in advance. Normally there's no objection if they know who wants to see the lot, and if he's willing to pay all the postage and insurance, and get everything back inside of 24 hours. But Morris got quite mysterious about the whole thing, wouldn't tell his client's name or anything else about him. Except that as far as Morris knew, he was an outsider. So being a conservative house, naturally, they apologized and said no."

"What do you think?" said Oedipa, already knowing pretty much.

"That our mysterious bidder may be from Tristero," Cohen said. "And saw the description of the lot in the auction catalogue. And wants to keep evidence that Tristero exists out of unauthorized hands. I wonder what kind of a price they'll offer."

Oedipa went back to Echo Courts to drink bourbon until the sun went down and it was as dark as it would ever get. Then she went out and drove on the freeway for a while with her lights out, to see what would happen. But angels were watching. Shortly after midnight she found herself in a phone booth, in a desolate, unfamiliar, unlit district of San Narciso. She put in a station call to The Greek Way in San Francisco, gave the musical voice that answered a description of the acned, fuzz-headed Inamorato Anonymous she'd talked to there and waited, inexplicable tears beginning to build up pressure around her eyes. Half a minute of clinking glasses, bursts of laughter, sounds of a juke box. Then he came on.

"This is Arnold Snarb," she said, choking up.

"I was in the little boys' room," he said. "The men's room was full."

She told him, quickly, using up no more than a minute, what she'd learned about The Tristero, what had happened to Hilarius, Mucho, Metzger, Driblette, Fallopian. "So you are," she said, "the only one I have. I don't know your name, don't want to. But I have to know whether they arranged it with you. To run into me by accident, and tell me your story about the post horn. Because it may be a practical joke for you, but it stopped being one for me a few hours ago. I got drunk and went driving on these freeways. Next time I may be more deliberate. For the love of God, human life, whatever you respect, please. Help me."

"Arnold," he said. There was a long stretch of bar noise.

"It's over," she said, "they've saturated me. From here on I'll only close them out. You're free. Released. You can tell me."

"It's too late," he said.

"For me?"

"For me." Before she could ask what he meant, he'd hung up. She had no more coins. By the time she could get somewhere to break a bill, he'd be gone. She stood between the public booth and the rented car, in the night, her isolation complete, and tried to face toward the sea. But she'd lost her bearings. She turned, pivoting on one stacked heel, could find no mountains either. As if there could be no barriers between herself and the rest of the land. San Narciso at that moment lost (the loss pure, instant, spherical, the sound of a stainless orchestral chime held among the stars and struck lightly), gave up its residue of uniqueness for her; became a name again, was assumed back into the American continuity of crust and mantle. Pierce Inverarity was really dead.

She walked down a stretch of railroad track next to the highway. Spurs ran off here and there into factory property. Pierce may have owned these factories too. But did it matter now if he'd owned all of San Narciso? San Narciso was a name; an incident among our climatic records of dreams and what dreams became among our accumulated daylight, a moment's squall-line or tornado's touchdown among the higher, more continental solemnities—storm-systems of group suffering and need, prevailing winds of affluence. There was the true continuity, San Narciso had no boundaries. No one knew yet how to draw them. She had dedicated herself, weeks ago, to making sense of what Inverarity had left behind, never suspecting that the legacy was America.

Might Oedipa Maas yet be his heiress; had that been in the will, in code, perhaps without Pierce really knowing, having been by then too seized by some headlong expansion of himself, some visit, some lucid instruction? Though she could never again call back any image of the dead man to dress up, pose, talk to and make answer, neither would she lose a new compassion for the cul-de-sac he'd tried to find a way out of, for the enigma his efforts had created.

Though he had never talked business with her, she had known it to be a fraction of him that couldn't come out even, would carry forever beyond any decimal place she might name; her love, such as it had been, remaining incommensurate with his need to possess, to alter the land, to bring new skylines, personal antagonisms, growth rates into being. "Keep it bouncing," he'd told her once, "that's all the secret, keep it bouncing." He must have known, writing the will, facing the spectre, how the bouncing would stop. He might have written the testament only to harass a one-time mistress, so cynically sure of being wiped out he could throw away all hope of anything more. Bitterness could have run that deep in him. She just didn't know. He might himself have discovered The Tristero, and encrypted that in the will, buying into just enough to be sure she'd find it. Or he might even have tried to survive death, as a paranoia; as a pure conspiracy against someone he loved. Would that breed of perversity prove at last too keen to be stunned even by death, had a plot finally been devised too elaborate for the dark Angel to hold at once, in his humorless vice-president's head, all the possibilities of? Had something slipped through and Inverarity by that much beaten death?

Yet she knew, head down, stumbling along over the cinder-bed and its old sleepers, there was still that other chance. That it was all true. That Inverarity had only died, nothing else. Suppose, God, there really was a Tristero then and that she *had* come on it by accident. If San Narciso and the estate were really no different from any other town, any other estate, then by that continuity she might have found The Tristero anywhere in her Republic, through any of a hundred lightly-concealed entranceways, a hundred alienations, if only she'd looked. She stopped a minute between the steel rails, raising her head as if to sniff the air. Becoming conscious of the hard, strung presence she stood on— knowing as if maps had been flashed for her on the sky how these tracks ran on into others, others, knowing they laced, deepened, authenticated the great night around her. If only she'd looked. She remembered now old Pullman cars, left where the money'd run out or the customers vanished, amid green farm flatnesses where clothes hung, smoke lazed out of jointed pipes. Where the squatters there in touch with others, through Tristero; were they helping carry forward that 300 years of the house's disinheritance? Surely they'd forgotten by now what it was the Tristero were to have inherited; as perhaps Oedipa one day might have. What was left to inherit? That America coded in Inverarity's testament, whose was that? She thought of other, immobilized freight cars, where the kids sat on the floor planking and sang back, happy as fat, whatever came over the mother's pocket radio; of other squatters who stretched canvas for lean-tos behind smiling billboards along all the highways, or slept in junkyards in the stripped shells of wrecked Plymouths, or even, daring, spent the night up some pole in a lineman's tent like caterpillars, swung among a web of telephone wires, living in the very copper rigging and secular miracle of communication, untroubled by the dumb voltages flickering their miles, the night long, in the thousands of unheard messages. She remembered drifters she had listened to, Americans speaking their language carefully, scholarly, as if they were in exile from somewhere else invisible yet congruent with the cheered land she lived in; and walkers along the roads at night, zooming in and out of your headlights without looking up, too far from any town to have a real destination. And the voices before and after the dead man's that had phoned at random during the darkest, slowest hours, searching ceaseless among the dial's ten million possibilities for that magical Other who would reveal herself out of the roar of relays, monotone litanies of insult, filth, fantasy, love whose brute repetition must someday call into being the trigger for the unnamable act, the recognition, the Word.

How many shared Tristero's secret, as well as its exile? What would the probate judge have to say about spreading some kind of a legacy among them all, all those nameless, maybe as a first installment? Oboy. He'd be on her ass in a microsecond, revoke her letters testamentary, they'd call her names, proclaim her through all Orange County as a redistributionist and pinko, slip the old man from Warpe, Wistfull, Kubitschek and McMingus in as administrator *de bonis non* and so much baby for code, constellations, shadowlegatees. Who knew? Perhaps she'd be hounded someday as far as joining Tristero itself, if it existed, in its twilight, its aloofness, its waiting. The waiting above all; if not for another set of possibilities to replace those that had conditioned the land to accept any San Narciso among its most tender flesh without a reflex or a cry, then at least, at the very least, waiting for a symmetry of choices to break down, to go skew. She had heard all about excluded middles; they were bad shit, to be avoided; and how had it ever happened here, with the chances once so good for diversity? For it was now like walking among matrices of a great digital computer, the zeroes and ones twinned above, hanging like balanced mobiles right and left, ahead, thick, maybe endless. Behind the hieroglyphic streets there would either be a transcendent meaning, or only the earth. In the songs Miles, Dean, Serge and Leonard sang was either some fraction of the truth's numinous beauty (as Mucho now believed) or only a power spectrum. Tremaine the Swastika Salesman's reprieve from holocaust was either an injustice, or the absence of a wind; the bones of the GI's at the bottom of Lake Inverarity were there either for a reason that mattered to the world, or for skin divers and cigarette smokers. Ones and zeroes. So did the couples arrange themselves. At Vesperhaven House either an accommodation reached, in some kind of dignity, with the Angel of Death, or only death and the daily, tedious preparations for it. Another mode of meaning behind the obvious, or none. Either Oedipa in the orbiting ecstasy of a true paranoia, or a real Tristero. For there either was some Tristero beyond the appearance of the legacy America, or there was just America and if there was just America then it seemed the only was she could continue, and manage to be at all relevant to it, was as an alien, unfurrowed, assumed full circle into some paranoia.

Next day, with the courage you find you have when there is nothing more to lose, she got in touch with C. Morris Schrift, and inquired after his mysterious client.

"He decided to attend the auction in person," was all Schrift would tell her. "You might run into him there." She might.

The auction was duly held, on a Sunday afternoon, in perhaps the oldest building in San Narciso, dating from before World War II. Oedipa arrived a few minutes early, alone, and in a cold lobby of gleaming redwood floorboards and the smell of wax and paper, she met Genghis Cohen, who looked genuinely embarrassed.

"Please don't call it a conflict of interests," he drawled earnestly. "There were some lovely Mozambique triangles I couldn't quite resist. May I ask if you've come to bid, Miz Maas."

"No," said Oedipa, "I'm only being a busybody."

"We're in luck. Loren Passerine, the finest auctioneer in the West, will be crying today."

"Will be what?"

"We say an auctioneer 'cries' a sale," Cohen said.

"Your fly is open," whispered Oedipa. She was not sure what she'd do when the bidder revealed himself. She had only some vague idea about causing a scene violent enough to bring the cops into it and find out that way who the man really was. She stood in a patch of sun, among brilliant rising and falling points of dust, trying to get a little warm, wondering if she'd go through with it.

"It's time to start," said Genghis Cohen, offering his arm. The men inside the auction room wore black mohair and had pale, cruel faces. They watched her come in, trying each to conceal his thoughts. Loren Passerine, on his podium, hovered like a puppet-master, his eyes bright, his smile practiced and relentless. He stared at her, smiling, as if saying, I'm surprised you actually came. Oedipa sat alone, toward the back of the room, looking at the napes of necks, trying to guess which one was her target, her enemy, perhaps her proof. An assistant closed the heavy door on the lobby windows and the sun. She heard a lock snap shut; the sound echoed a moment. Passerine spread his arms in a gesture that seemed to belong to the priesthood of some remote culture; perhaps to a descending angel. The auctioneer cleared his throat. Oedipa settled back, to await the crying of lot 49.

BOOKS BY THOMAS PYNCHON

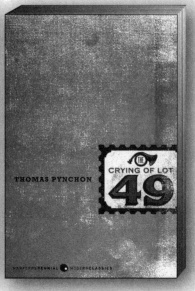

V.

ISBN 0-06-093021-7

Winner of the coveted William Faulkner Foundation First Novel Award in 1963, *V.* is a wild, macabre, modernist tale of the twentieth century at the center of which are two men (one looking for something he has lost; the other with nothing to lose) and a mysterious woman known only as "V."

"Filled with wild humor, inventive wordplay, and a darkly imaginative power."　*—Philadelphia Inquirer*

"[*V.*] leaves the imagination spent and the mind reeling."
　　—New York Herald Tribune

THE CRYING OF LOT 49

ISBN 0-06-0931671

Oedipa Maas is made the executor of the estate of her late boyfriend, Pierce Inverarity. As she diligently carries out her duties, Oedipa is enmeshed in what would appear to be a worldwide conspiracy, meets some extremely interesting characters, and attains a not-inconsiderable amount of self-knowledge.

"The work of a virtuoso with prose. . . . His intricate symbolic order [is] akin to that of Joyce's *Ulysses*."
—Chicago Tribune